THE TALLEST MAN IN TEXAS

Some men have it in them to stand out in any crowd. And Ben Allison was unquestionably such a man.

Six-four if he was an inch, he was all bone and sinew fattened by nothing but snake muscle—and he was one quarter Comanche. His face was lean and dark, while his long hair was a pale, flax blond where it swept from beneath the flat-crowned black hat.

Men first meeting him looked at one another, shrugged, called him slow. It was an obvious judgment.

But in Texas, men who had seen him move no longer called Ben Allison slow . . .

THE
TALL
MEN

Clay Fisher

BANTAM BOOKS
TORONTO · NEW YORK · LONDON · SYDNEY

*This low-priced Bantam Book
has been completely reset in a type face
designed for easy reading, and was printed
from new plates. It contains the complete
text of the original hard-cover edition.*
NOT ONE WORD HAS BEEN OMITTED.

THE TALL MEN

*A Bantam Book / published by arrangement with
Clay Fisher*

PRINTING HISTORY

Houghton Mifflin edition published 1954

Bantam edition / September 1970

2nd printing ...... July 1971	4th printing ..... April 1975
3rd printing ...... June 1972	5th printing ... January 1982

*Bantam Books are published by Bantam Books, Inc. Its trade-
mark, consisting of the words "Bantam Books" and the por-
trayal of a rooster, is Registered in U.S. Patent and Trademark
Office and in other countries. Marca Registrada. Bantam
Books, Inc., 666 Fifth Avenue, New York, New York 10103.*

PRINTED IN THE UNITED STATES OF AMERICA

14 13 12 11 10 9 8 7 6 5

Chapter One

THEY CAME from the south, riding ahead of the February twilight. Where the stage road crossed the last of the brooding hills they pulled their horses in. They sat them in silence, staring long into the valley below.

Two miles down the gulch, beyond the main settlement, could be seen the lights of a second town. And beyond that, those of a third.

The two riders shook their heads, moved uneasily in their saddles.

They were lonely, wandering men, little taken with the ways of civilization and having, by hard reason of professional calling, ample cause for caution in regard to those ways. The year was 1866, the war nearly twelve months over. Lately they had been soldiers and before that, cowboys. But they had come home to find the herds scattered, the ranches deserted, the owners departed. Bread was no longer to be earned, nor board provided, by the practice of their sole art —the care and feeding of longhorn cattle on the open range.

But the belly, in particular the ravenous, demanding belly of youth, had to be filled.

In the following hunt to fill that belly it was inevitable that the old profession be replaced by the new. The war had taught them one proficiency. That of the gun. Within sixty days of Appomattox they were in business.

It had proved a poor one.

Along the Smokey Hill and Santa Fe stage roads which traversed their native Texas and Indian Territory heath, paying stage traffic was still but a trickle. And the hostile Kiowas and Cheyennes, grown overbold through the four-year absence of the Union troops, were shutting that trickle down to a starvation drip. Shortly it became impossible for an honest young road agent to earn a decent living.

At this turn, hopeful word filtered down from the north. The gold strikes were still continuing in the country of Grasshopper Creek, Bannack and the Last Chance. It was information which caused the two youthful businessmen to look toward the land of the Sioux and the prospect of paying color at the grassroots with a cool and calculating eye.

Where there was gold in the ground there would be men to

dig it out. Those men would be wearing pants and those pants would have pockets. Before long that gold would wind up in those pockets. Men with gold in their pockets were apt to travel. Where they were, other men with no gold in their pockets were apt to gather.

The two riders upon the hill had no gold in their pockets.

"So thet's her," the first rider said at last. "Ben, she makes Fort Worth look like a cowtown."

"Fort Worth *is* a cowtown," said the second rider.

He made the statement simply and without apparent imagination, as a schoolboy would say Iowa is noted for her corn, or the Mississippi River begins in the north and ends in the south.

He was a man who saw things that way.

The sun rose in the east, sank in the west. Water flowed downhill, a tree bent to the wind, grass grew in the spring.

It was what fooled you about Ben Allison. Men first meeting him looked at one another superiorly, shrugged, called him slow. It was an obvious judgment and one with which Ben seldom argued. But in the Southwest where he had come from men who had seen him move no longer called Ben Allison slow.

"But this ain't Fort Worth," he continued now to his companion, breaking the long, thoughtful pause, "and it ain't no cowtown."

"It sure ain't!" agreed the other fervently. "Though I wish to Gawd it was. This here north wind has got my Dixie backside shakin' like a hounddawg passin' peach seeds. Let's ride on down before we're froze solid."

"All right, we're gone. Mind you now, Clint, don't be callin' me Ben once we're down yonder, you hear?" With the warning, he put his black gelding down the hillside, Clint following him.

"Sure. What'll it be this time?" Clint was cold and hungry and long without whiskey. And tired of changing names every time they rode over a new hill.

"I think I'll be 'Sam' this time," grinned Ben good-naturedly. "Sam Allen. Say mebbe fer full, Sam Houston Allen."

"Ain't thet a little fancy fer *you?*"

"Could be I'm feelin' a little fancy."

"Fair enough." Clint returned the slow grin. "I'll be Tom. Tom Pickett. Tom Jefferson Davis Pickett. Thet flossy enough fer you, sport?"

Ben nodded soberly, accepting the other's Mason and

2

Dixon alias. "Yonder's the town," he gestured, reining his pony to a walk. "Now remember, bud, you see you don't leave your liquor do your talkin' fer you." He paused, eying the younger man. "You hear me, Clint Allison?"

"You handle your load, I'll handle mine," said his brother shortly.

Again Ben nodded.

"All right, Clint, you're a man growed. You know why we're here and what we come fer. It ain't fer fun and it ain't fer whiskey. Nor," he added meaningfully, "fer women."

"Hard work," announced Clint straightfaced. "Thet's what makes the world go round. Lead on, good brother."

They turned the corner of Wallace and Van Buren Streets, squinting to the sudden blaze of the full city lights.

The first things as always with such camps were the saloons. Slowing their horses they read them off: the Shades, the Big Horn, Barney Bailey's, the Black Nuggett—as many as a dozen others. There seemed no end to them, nor to the brawling mill of loud-voiced, bearded miners crowding their entrances.

"Good Gawd Amighty," muttered Clint, "lookit all them cussed muckers and powder monkeys. I never see sech a herd of hardrock gophers in my life."

"What'd you expect?" asked Ben slowly. "Cowboys? This here is Montana, son. Gold is what they grow here, not beef."

"I reckon it is," said Clint wonderingly. "But I cain't gentle myse'f to it. Man, I allowed I'd seen some sizable diggin's in my time, but this here—good Gawd Amighty!"

"Diggin's come and diggin's go," nodded Ben quietly. "But they don't come no bigger nor go no richer than Virginia City—"

They left their horses at Bailey's corral. As they stepped into the outer glare of the street, they paused in the shadows of the stable alley only long enough to check their business assets. There was no conversation. They eased the long Colts from their half-frozen leathers, checked the capping of the nipples, eased the weapons back into the low holsters beneath the threadbare gray of the Confederate-issue cavalry overcoats.

"Don't fergit, Clint," Ben grunted, "right off we do nothin'. Jest look and listen and size up our best bet."

"I want a circuit rider, I'll send fer you," growled Clint impatiently. "Right now my belly's yellin' fer sourmash, not sermons. Let's drift."

"All right, watch yerse'f. Leave me do the talkin'."

"It's a deal." Clint stepped out of the alley. "I'll do the drinkin'."

Ben watched him a minute, narrow-eyed, then hunched his shoulders and moved after him into the surge of the street crowd. Clint was a handful when the wind blew from where the women wore stockings and the city lights came served up with a bottle of forty rod. Sweet as a desert peach, sober, he was a pure crazy Comanche, drunk.

Likely, Ben had always figured, it was their Indian grandmother showing up in him. For when you used that word Comanche on Clint, you weren't more than three quarters fooling. The old lady had been a fullblood Kwanhadi. That red blood was strong, especially when mixed with the Virginia and Tennessee mountain strain which lay back of his and Clint's dad.

Nobody in God's green world, excepting maybe Ben, could push Clint an inch once he'd got started on the Taos Lightning. He could hold more than a charred oak barrel and looked to see no higher reward in this life than setting out to prove it at the first pop of a quart stopper.

Well, that had been fine for the old days when they were cowboys and had ridden into Lampasas or Paint Rock to tie one on. But the old days were long gone. The cow business as he and Clint had known it before the war would never come back. Nor would West Texas. The North Concho and San Saba country no longer had any more use for cowboys than it did for cows. And never would again. Meantime, in the tight game they were playing there was no room for whiskey. When you made your living with a gun you shot from taw, bare knuckles flat, and you didn't play for chalkies. And when you checked your cylinders on the way to work, you never poured your powder from a bottle.

Shouldering through the polygot human ore of Virginia City's mainstreet vein, Ben caught up with the restless, long-striding Clint.

"We'll hit the Black Nugget, first." He sidemouthed his orders. "She's hooked onto the hotel and looks to be drawin' the flashiest crowd."

"Lead on, brother!" Clint's quicksilver character shifted to the spread of the big grin. "Our few bucks ain't goin' to last no longer in thet plush parlor than a Kansas darkie in a Ken-

4

tucky crap game. But I'm your man, Sam. Jest show me the way!"

"Clint," said Ben slowly, "happen you don't wash out on me, I'll likely show you more than the way." He paused, his eyes looking through and past his brother and far away, as they had a habit of doing to a man when that sober-dark mind of his was turning on a thought. "I got a hunch we're goin' to make the biggest strike since Comstock stumbled on his lode in Six-Mile Canyon."

In his quiet, slow way, unknown to himself or Clint or any man then living, Ben Allison spoke in words as tall as the shadow of history itself.

Chapter Two

THERE WERE UPWARD of a hundred men packed into the forty-foot square of the Black Nugget's main mud-floored saloon. From among their sardined ranks the practiced eye of the bartender picked the two newcomers the moment the street doors swung inward to admit them.

His swift glance of discovery was followed by a second look, equally practiced, toward the bar's undercounter and the rusted, ten-gauge shotgun which rested there. Satisfied, he returned his gaze to the approaching customers, nodding to himself as he did so. These were sure enough ten-gauge birds. And tough as buckshot.

Some men have it in them to stand out in any crowd. Unquestionably, these were such men.

The first one was very tall, blackhaired, noticeably slant of eye and easy of grin. Any boy long enough in a gold camp to know a jackhammer from a bullprod drill would know this one was no miner.

The second man was taller still, six-four if he was an inch, and all bone and sinew fattened by nothing but snake muscle. His face was different too, not so fresh nor so startlingly handsome, leaner and skullier than the first man's, while his long hair was a pale, flax blond where it swept from beneath the flat-crowned black hat. But in the end it was the eyes which set the two apart for you.

Where the first man's were a deep, raw sky blue, those of the second were so light and springwater cold as to be almost colorless. And slitted as they were above the high cheekbones, watchful and wolf thoughtful, they trapped you and held you while those of his companion merely tapped you on the shoulder going by.

"What do they drink in Montana, friend?"

It was the second man asking it, the one with the eyes. His voice was pleasant and easy as March wind in a silver thaw. It fooled a man and made him uneasy.

"Valley Tan. Four bits a shot, eight dollars a bottle," grumbled the bartender, suddenly finding his bar top in need of a nervous polishing.

"Make it a bottle and two glasses."

Clint scowled at Ben's order. "What's the idee? I had it in mind to belly-up to the bar."

"You had it in mind to get stunk-up as a skunk, too. But you ain't. Yonder's a corner table jest cleared. Grab the whiskey."

Clint speared the bottle out of the bartender's hand, strode angrily off. Ben carefully counted the eight silver dollars onto the bar, frowned at what it left him and followed Clint. At the table he spun the last silver cartwheel toward his brother. "Don't spend it all in one place," he grunted.

"Gawd Amighty," grinned Clint, the prospect of the whiskey lifting his spirits, "you mean we're thet close to the blanket?"

"Thet's all there is, there ain't no more," said Ben. "Drink up."

The younger Allison half filled his pint tumbler, slid the bottle and the other glass to Ben. His drink was down before Ben's was poured. The subsequent stiffening of his scalp hair nearly lifted his hat off his head but he only gazed speculatively into the bottom of his empty glass and announced gently, "Watch thet first mouthful, brother. It's a seven-day son of a bitch."

Ben poured three fingers, put them down.

"It ain't been in the barrel long," he agreed.

"Thet stuff never saw no barrel," said Clint. "They bottled it right out'n the buffler wallow, bull-water and all."

"Likely," nodded Ben, looking around the room. "You see anything thet looks good to you?"

"Thet strawberry blonde yonder at the bar. The one with the million dollar nuggets."

Ben glanced at the blonde, scowled at his brother. Clint got the point, settled down.

"There's plenty of money in sight," he said, filling his glass again while making the observation.

"Thet's jest the trouble," muttered Ben, letting his eyes run the smoky gamut of the nearby poker tables. "It's in sight."

"Where's your trouble in thet?" Clint pegged his third shot, the Valley Tan going down like water now that its first flame had cremated his throat beyond all feeling. His older brother eyed him narrowly, saying nothing. Clint shrugged, poured his fourth glass. Ben let him finish, pulled the bottle away from him and held it up to the light.

"Thet'll be your pint."

He said it in a passing way but it was a statement, not an opinion. "What we're lookin' fer," he continued softly, "is a belt player. One with his poke in his pocket, not spilled out in front of him backin' a busted flush."

Clint looked at him, broke his eyes away, grinned, jerked his head toward the street doors. "Them as asks, gits," he drawled.

Ben watched the big man come in through the doors, pause inside them to scan the room as though looking for someone—or anyone. He nodded, not answering Clint, his eyes busy with the newcomer.

He was a blond man, one of the pinkskinned ones that never took a tan no matter they were in the sun and the wind their whole lives. And this one had been. You could tell that in a minute. He had a square of shoulders and trimming of hips for all his bulk, that told you right off he was a horseman. Not a cowboy nor yet a highline rider like him and Clint. But a man that knew horses and had sat to them one way or another, to ride or drive, for a long, tough spell.

Probably a freighter, thought Ben. But not driving any more. No working skinner wore buckskins like that, all fringe and handmade, nor boots of that slim, thin cut either. Those were genuine Cordovans, mister, and a man didn't come by a set of them for less than forty dollars, Yank. Clint had called this one's tune pure and clear.

He was their man.

The thought no sooner formed than Ben felt the impact of the newcomer's eyes. The big man's glance had found him in the crowd and fastened on him with a jolt he felt clear across the room. Then, even as Ben was returning the compliment and while the big man was turning away from the exchange of hard looks, a hoarse-voiced miner at the table next to his and Clint's was speaking disgustedly.

"There he is now. The big jasper in the buckskins and dude boots."

"Naw!" one of the miner's tablemates said incredulously.

"It's him," growled a third man. "The lucky bastard. It's jest like Jake says. He buys thet wuthless Yeller Jacket diggin's fer five-hundred dollars, hits a new pocket in three days, takes out thirty-thousand dollars in dust and hauls out clean this here very afternoon."

"Wonder what he's doin' in the Nugget?" said the second man, unconvinced. "Strikes me he's a purty fancy cat to be prowlin' this here kind of a alley."

"Reckon I kin tell you thet, too," nodded Jake superiorly. "He's clearin' out of Virginy City. Goin' down inter Texas somewheres. Got some kind of a crazy scheme he ain't talkin'

8

about. Says he'll make a million out of it inside three years and without he touches pick or pan the livelong time. I allow he's here to swap his dust fer greenbacks with old Lazarus. See, yonder he goes, headin' fer that goddam little green door."

Esau Lazarus, owner of the Black Nugget and half a dozen other saloons in Nevada City and Bannack down the gulch, was the camp money changer and self-established First National Bank of Virginia City. When a man with a floursack full of highgrade headed for his "little green door" behind the Nugget's backbar, it didn't take a financial genius to guess his business.

"What in hell's the exchange runnin' now?" scowled the second miner.

"Forty-to-thirty, bills fer dust," said Jake disgustedly. "It ain't changed since the first of the year."

"Well, there's a cramp nobody never cussed about survivin'," shrugged his companion. "Forty thousand dollars ain't too sharp a pain to take on. Not even in depreciated bills—"

By this time the oily mists of the Valley Tan were clearing even from Clint's narrowing eyes. He eased back in his chair, watching Ben.

The latter was methodically pouring the last of the whiskey into his tumbler. The downslanted tilt of his hatbrim indicated he had no other interest in the world. But beneath that brim his pale eyes were tracking the recent owner of the Yellow Jacket through the crowd and toward the green door, moving as soft padding, close and sure behind him as a mountain lion walking down a weanling colt.

"Git the hosses," he said to Clint. "Tie mine out front. When he leaves, you head him. I'll tail him out from in here."

"Anythin' else?" grinned Clint, coming to his feet.

"Yeah," said Ben softly. "Trust in the Lord and keep your finger on the trigger."

"*Aye de mi!*" sighed Clint, reverently palming his hands with the old Spanish phrase. "I do admire a humble, God-fearin' man."

The big man came out of Lazarus's office ten minutes after Clint had gone. Ben followed him to the street doors, watching him across their slatted tops. To a graybearded miner just entering, he drawled. "Say, pardner, who's the good-lookin' feller gettin' on the bay yonder?"

The oldster glanced toward the hitching rack. When he

looked back at Ben there was a shade of tightness at his eye corners.

He shifted his quid of longleaf Burley, spat through the doors.

"Well, now," he announced at length, "you might say he buys and sells minin' claims. And again you might say he runs the Guv'mint freight contract 'tween here and Fort Leavenworth, down to Kansas." His crowfooted eyes squinted along the entire six feet of Ben, from Texas boot-soles to traildusted black hat. "And still again, young un, you might say he's the head of the Virginy City Vigilantes."

He paused, eying the lean rider with the full relish of an old hardrock hand about to touch off a five-foot drillhole packed solid with prime grade DuPont powder.

"Think it over, son," he nodded slowly. *"That there's Nathan Stark."*

For all the outward effect the name had on Ben Allison, it might as well have been John Smith.

Inwardly, it hit him like a balled fist.

He and Clint hadn't been in the trade long. But they had ridden enough of its ridges to hear the names of a few of the past masters in the profession. Names like Frank Parrish, Ned Ray, Jack Gallegher, Boone Helm, George Ives and Henry Plummer.

And names like Nathan Stark.

The elevating part, of course, was not those first names, themselves, but their association with the last one. From first to last, beginning with George Ives and running through Boone Helm to Henry Plummer, the owner of each and every one of those famous outlaw labels had wound up on the necktie end of a Virginia City vigilante rope—by personal courtesy of Nathan Stark.

"Never heard of him," shrugged Ben. He added one of his sober grins to the dismissal, touching his hatbrim respectfully to the grizzled miner. "I'm beholden to you, nonetheless, oldtimer. See you down the trail."

"We ain't travelin' the same one," grunted the old man, and turned away.

Chapter Three

BEN SAW CLINT siding his sorrel mare in a shadow across the street. He had his head down, his shoulder in the saddle fenders, fussing with a cinchbuckle that just wouldn't seem to notch up right. At the Black Nugget rail, Nathan Stark was legging up on his bay. One look at the horse told you how near you'd been when you figured Stark for a horseman.

That bay was a Kentucky blooded horse, as fine in head as a jade cameo, as deep in barrel and haunch as a mountain grizzly. He was an uncut stud, the kind of a horse nobody but a *hombre duro* could have under him—and keep there.

But Nathan Stark was the one to ride him, and a hard man for all his pink cheeks and fine blue eyes.

If your look at him in the Nugget hadn't told you that, your look at his Kentucky studhorse was telling it to you now.

He waited for him to swing the stud clear of the rail, head him up the street, north, toward the short, dark edge of town, away from the down-gulch lights of Bannack and Nevada City. It was a good break and Ben grinned. Had he turned south, through the lower camps, it would have been only a two-bit chance they could have boxed him without they were seen at it and a respectable chunk of hell jacked up and raised right then and there. As it was, he apparently had his tent or cabin in the hills to the north. Five minutes would see all the darkness between him and Virginia City a man could ask for.

With the grin, Ben held up yet another handful of seconds, making sure Clint moved out on schedule. He did, sending the sorrel past Stark at just the right unhurried lope. The minute Clint had him headed, Ben went for his black.

The last saloon fell behind, the sagebrush and the starlight took over. The four or five inches of late, fresh snow on the ground opened up the darkness just enough to let a man see what he was doing—not enough to let other men see him doing it.

Stark was playing it just right, holding his bay on a slow jog about a hundred yards up on Ben. Ahead of him, Clint was picking up his sorrel's lope, opening up the ground between him and Stark. Straining the dim light of the trail ahead of Clint, Ben saw why.

Perhaps fifty yards north of where Clint had touched up

the sorrel, the trail angled sharply to the left, following the creekbed through a cutbank about ten feet high, not over twice that, wide.

Ben's lips straightened.

He kneed the black, edging his swift singlefoot up another notch. Clint knew the right spot when he saw it. And he had just seen it.

It worked the way you always dreamed they should—and almost never did. Stark was halfway through the watercut when Clint's mare loomed in front of him. He had no more than time to pull the bay in to avoid colliding with Clint when Ben's soft voice took over from behind.

"You're boxed, Mr. Stark. Point and drag."

"Hold that bay in," added Clint. "And don't use your hands fer nothin' but doin' it."

Nathan Stark was no stranger to dark nights and narrow trails. "He's held," he said quietly.

"Get his guns," ordered Ben. "Check him close for a Henry D."

Clint nodded. He slipped Stark's Colts out of their leathers, tossed them aside. His practiced hand slid inside the fringed jacket, quickly pulled away. "No Henry D." he grunted.

It was Ben's turn to nod. With Stark's fancy dressing kind you always looked for one of Henry Derringer's little pepperbox pistols stashed away somewhere inside. It was Rule One. Many a fine boy had taken a .41-caliber round ball through the brisket for his failure to observe it.

"Moneybelt?" he asked Clint.

"And fat," drawled the latter. "Greasy as a June grouse."

"Unhook it," Ben advised Stark. "Pass it to my friend. *Real slow.*"

Stark removed the belt. Clint took it, dropping it around his saddlehorn with his free left hand. His Colt-filled right never left the target area of Stark's solar plexus.

To the moment, Ben had been behind the Virginia City man. Now he moved the black gelding around him.

"We like it clean and quiet, Mr. Stark. It works best for everybody. You been real nice. We're some taken with your company."

"You have the money," said Nathan Stark dourly. "Get out of my way and let me go on."

"I reckon you didn't understand me, Mr. Stark. I said we was taken with your company. Fact is, we're that taken with it we dassn't leave it."

"Have your little joke," gritted Nathan Stark. "You can afford it, I believe."

"He ain't jokin', mister." Clint let the advice come earnestly. "He don't know how."

"What do you want of me, you scoundrels? You have my money. If you mean to take my life as well, get on with it."

"'Pears you're in a tolerable stampede to git to hell," observed Clint. "I allow we won't hold you up none. Move jest a shade to the side, Samuel."

Ben held the black right where he was.

The interesting thing about Clint was that he forever kept a man on his toes. Never a dull moment with old Clint. Half grin or whole, pleasant nod or airy salutation, cheerful greeting, warm advice, sagacious counsel or spiritual solicitude, it was all the same with Clint. And always the same. The voice stayed soft, the eyes innocent, the mouth loose and friendly. And you were left to try and guess what in God's name he would do next.

Right now Ben was guessing that if he moved the black one hip-switch away from in front of Nathan Stark, Clint would kill him.

And Stark wasn't helping any.

"Hell be damned!" said the Virginia City man, boldly. "Get on with it. I don't fear you."

"Now, I reckon it ain't that desp'rit," soothed Ben, heeling the black deliberately into Clint's mare, not liking the way the latter was edging her clear. "It's jest that it's a fine night fer a ride and we'd admire to have you jine us." The drawl dropped a tone. "Move that bay along, Mr. Stark."

"I'll not move him an inch, you understand? You have what you came for, now get out." He paused, eying them both, levelly. "It would be my final suggestion that you get *far* out."

Ben studied him.

"Mr. Stark," he said at last, and speculatively, "we have been here before. We can count to ten without our fingers."

"So?" The belligerency was unabated.

"So, we don't ride off in a strange country and let you bust back into the Black Nugget ten minutes after we follow you out of it."

"Naturally," Clint eased the suggestion in, "I'm in favor of leavin' you here. And if my friend Sam will git out'n the way—"

"Hold that mare still!" Ben broke him off, low voiced, and

13

Clint checked his sorrel, along with his request. But Stark continued to make it tough.

"I don't scare worth a damn, boys, so save your breath for fighting the rope." He sat relaxed in the saddle, not moving to obey Ben's order to get going and not knuckling to Clint's drawling implication as to how things would fare with him if he didn't. If he was bluffing, Ben thought, he was almighty easy about it.

He decided he wasn't.

"We don't want to leave you here," he said. "I'd ruther we didn't *need* to." He caught the big man's look and held it. "I reckon it ain't no longer a case of nobody bein' afraid of nobody, Mr. Stark. I'll give you that."

"And I'll give you five seconds," said Clint. "And start countin' at three. My friend is soft in the haid. I ain't. You comin' or stayin', mister?"

Nathan Stark looked long at both riders. He took all of Clint's five seconds. And in the end he nodded.

"It's a better night than I thought. Let's go."

"Two's company," grunted Clint. "I'll ride point. Whereaway, Samuel?" With the grunt and as a matter of standard past procedure, he handed the moneybelt to Ben.

"South, along the base of the hills." Ben took the belt. "I allow we'd best hook back up with the road we came in on, seein's we don't know no other." He pulled the black off the trail, touching his hat to Nathan Stark.

"After you, Mr. Stark—"

Nathan Stark said no more. He swung his horse in behind Clint's, following the latter's mount out of the creekbed gully and on up the steep slope of the flanking hill beyond. Behind him came Ben.

Only the quease and squeak of the freezing saddles and the grunting slosh of the water in the stomach of Stark's bay broke the stillness. Occasionally a striking forefoot, slashing the crusted surface snow for the surer footing of the rock beneath it, would ring the night with the thin sound of iron on granite. But that was all. There was no more talk and no more need for talk. The sheerness of the climb and the glare-ice treachery of the trail Clint picked up and across it left no spare eye nor effort for conversation.

And the lateness of the hour, for all concerned, left no time for it.

Two gaunt riders from fifteen hundred miles south had highwayed and hoisted the foremost citizen of the toughest mining camp west of Denver or north of Laramie. Two lean

14

gentlemen from Texas, plyers of a trade which their silent guest had stamped out in Montana with twenty-two hangings in six weeks, had their wolf by the tail and knew it.

There was one way out for them and they were taking it.

To Ben and Clint Allison it was only interesting, and beside any point of personal fear, that they were sharing that way with the fabled head of Virginia City's dread vigilantes. With a gun in their guts, all men were equal.

And they had a gun in Nathan Stark's guts.

Chapter Four

ON TOP OF the divide over which the stage road came into Virginia City from the south, they pulled their horses in. While their mounts rested, the minds of their three riders did not.

Clint thought of the $40,000 in terms of blondes and bourbon. Ben thought of it in measures of the trail ahead, how to ride it to put the most of Montana they could between them and Virginia City before daylight, and how to ride it in the futureless months and miles that would follow that bleak northern sunrise. Nathan Stark thought of it along lines of coldblooded calculation—the odds against his chances of getting it back by betting his brains against their guns.

Nathan Stark never gambled, he only took chances. The difference was that between a busted flush and a businessman. He had come out of the east ten years before, an eighteen-year-old farm lad without a penny in his patched jeans. He had built a solid future for himself in that decade and men called him a gambler for it. They called him wrong. He played the percentages, always, and he never bet against the house. And when he played, he did so with the bluest of all chips—*brains*.

Nathan Stark had a mind like a steel trap, all honed teeth and coiled springs. When that mind snapped shut on something, it never let it go again. Weeks before, it had closed on the thought of bringing beef to Montana's meat-hungry mining camps. And only an hour gone, it had rung instantly shut on the one thing lacking to bring that thought into the hard focus of reality—the lean, trailwise, wolfwary form of Ben Allison.

He had had the gaunt Texan marked the minute he saw him. He knew the breed. Knew, too, a superlative specimen of it when he saw him. Only the necessity of first reaching camp and cacheing the bills he had gotten from Lazarus had kept him from approaching Ben in the Black Nugget. Now the game had gotten beyond the percentages he liked. And beyond the certainty he preferred. But not yet, not quite yet, beyond the limitless, last cunning of the calculated chance. And in the end, even as he pushed his first stack forward, he knew he was risking exactly nothing against $40,000.

"Boys," he announced, apparently speaking as much to the

wind and the snow as to either of them, "we're all in the same tight together. You figure it out."

They were his first words since the forty-five-minute climb began. Their unexpectedness pulled Ben around in his saddle.

"I been figgerin'," he said. "Mebbe the same as you, mebbe different. You're talkin'."

Stark nodded. "You've got twenty thousand dollars," he said slowly. "What do you mean to do with it?"

"What the hell you mean?" challenged Clint. "We was told forty thousand."

"I'm not talking to you," replied Stark, staring at him, jaw thrust. "I *know* what you'll do with your twenty thousand."

Ben grinned as Clint cursed.

This Nathan Stark was nobody's ninny. It was too bad they had met going opposite sides of the streambed. He would more than do to ride most rivers with. Especially if they were on the rise and over the willows.

"Keep talkin'," he shrugged. "We got a few minutes while the hosses blow. I allus aim to listen when a man makes sense."

"First off," said Stark, "the money's in big bills, mainly mint-fresh. You'll have to discount it say forty per cent to get rid of it, and have to ride to the Indian Territory or even to Mexico before you can do that well. That leaves you twelve thousand and you haven't bought a twist of Burley yet."

"Otherwise?" suggested Ben soberly.

"Otherwise, you'll start spending it the way it is and those new hundreds will hang along your backtrail like buzzards over a sick calf."

"And—?"

"You've heard of the Pinkertons?"

Ben had. His short nod conveyed the fact to Stark.

"In my time among the road agents," continued the Virginia City freighter pointedly, "I've had some small use for them now and again."

"So—?"

"They will be up to you," said Nathan Stark flatly, "before you've gotten shut of the first thousand."

It was no idle threat.

Ben knew it.

The Pinkerton National Detective Agency was the one bunch a man in his business did well not to deal with. Local sheriffs and even U.S. marshals could be bought off, or dodged, and in any event seldom stirred themselves after a man unless he was posted with a fat enough price. He and

17

Clint were new and not yet known. There wasn't a single flybill out on them, at least that they'd heard of, let alone a posted reward.

But the Pinkertons were something else again.

They had run the Union Army's Secret Service during the War between the States. Ben knew more than a little something about that from his fourteen months as a Union prisoner. They were a real, *organized* outfit. Once any customer of theirs put them on a man's trail, they never quit. Just as clearly as he was sitting there on his bay stud waiting for Ben's answer, Nathan Stark meant to put them after him and Clint.

"You're making it tough," he said at last. "We may have to 'leave you here' yet."

"You may rest assured, my friend, that I'm not intending to be 'left.' I'm not trying to make it tough, but tempting."

"Run them tracks another turn of the trail," said Ben.

"You're a Texan," nodded Stark. "And a cowman."

"You've been peekin'," interrupted Clint accusingly.

"So?" said Ben, ignoring his brother.

"So," said Stark, compounding the fraternal slight, "you know cattle, *and all there is to know about cattle.*"

"Go on."

"What were steers selling at when you left Texas?"

"They wasn't sellin'."

"Suppose somebody was buying?"

"Three, four dollars a head. All you want and buyer's pick and choice. What you gittin' at, Mr. Stark? You ain't makin' sense no more."

"The hosses are blowed." Clint was no longer affable nor easy. "We're movin'."

He ticked his mare with his Petmakers spurs, jumping her out of her head-down drowse. Ben clucked to his gelding, reined him around. "Let's go, Mr. Stark."

"Hold up, both of you!"

Stark jumped it at them, his excitement so real a man couldn't miss it. Sensing it, Ben checked the black.

"Boys," Stark swept on, shoving his last stack into the narrow opening of Ben's hesitation. "I'm making more sense than you've ever listened to in your lives. Get this—"

"Make it quick," snapped Clint. "And simple. Me and my frosted butt are gittin' quick-sick of both of you."

"Fortunately, my simple-minded friend," said Stark acidly, "I can make it short enough to span even your mental gap.

18

In Texas we buy three thousand cows for ten thousand dollars, in Montana we sell them for ninety thousand dollars."

"I got a even better idee," drawled Clint, loose grin returning with the thought, "In South Carolina we buy soft coal fer two bits a sack, and sell it to the Eskimos fer two dollars. Leggo my laig, mister, 'fore I jam my boot in yer mouth."

Ben had not even heard Clint's curdled reply. His held breath eased out now behind his slow realization of Stark's historic proposal. "Good Gawd Amighty," he murmured to the Virginia City man. "You fairly mean to drive a herd from Fort Worth to Virginia City!"

"I *did* mean to."

"It's your 'crazy scheme' we hear about in the Black Nugget. The one you wouldn't tell nobody." Ben's mind was already lost in the one world he knew and loved. The sagebrush, saddle leather, horse sweat, cow chip world of the Texas longhorn.

"It *was*." Stark left it short, sensing the excitement he had aroused in the southerner.

"Man," breathed Ben softly, "it *could be* done!"

"But by Gawd it ain't goin' to be!" barked Clint, knowing his older brother and knowing where his mind went the minute anybody wrote "cow" on the blackboard. "Goddamit, now—"

"Ease off," said Ben, his imagination caught up with a vision too big for Clint's. "How'd you see it workin', Mr. Stark?"

Quickly then, voice low, tense words drumming the darkness, Nathan Stark filled in his dream.

He told them of the Gallatin Valley, a stretch of grass bellydeep to the tallest longhorn ever calved. He told them of its cuts and draws and sheltered creek bottoms, and of a secret they held which no white man before him had learned—cattle could winter through on the open range in Montana.

He had suspected it from the beginning, had this past winter turned loose eighty head of worn-out workstock in a gamble against his hunch.

Those yoke-galled bulls had gone into the valley in September, thin and slatribbed and ready to drop. There had been blizzards in December and January, blizzards no stock could go through without stormsheds and hay corrals to hold them out of the wind and free of the snow. Ten days ago, with spring peeking over the Big Horns, he had ridden out to the Gallatin expecting to find a frozen ox every four miles from one end of its watershed to the other. Instead he had found the whole bunch, not a head missing and all grass-fat as open heifers in August, safe in a cross timbered creek draw!

He told them, then, of his planning of how it would work and what he would need. First, money. Lots of it. Then men. Many men. Texas men, who knew cattle and could take them where the devil himself, no matter he had hoofs and horns, wouldn't dare go. And one man, especially. The man who had already ridden the trail between the Alamo and Alder Gulch. The man who not only knew the way and knew cattle —but knew men.

The Texas cowboys could handle the herd.

But who would handle the Texas cowboys?

Clearly, there was one man alone who could do that and live to laugh about it.

Another Texan.

Then, quietly, Nathan Stark played his buried ace.

For this last man, this hoped for, all important trailboss, he, Stark, had planned an equal partnership in the Gallatin Valley ranch. *Fifty-fifty on every head that came through to Montana alive, and on every calf that was dropped in the Gallatin from then on until the tally book was closed!*

When he had finished, he sat his horse in silence, staring at Ben ahead of the final pause and nod.

"That man, my friend," he said slowly, "was going to be you."

Ben did not answer. His thoughts, funneled up into the whirlwind maw of Nathan Stark's imagination, were far from Montana. His eyes looked down upon the distant, twinkling lights of Virginia City and saw them not. His face burned to the keening bite of the high country's winter nightwind and failed to feel its sting. His ear listened to its lonely, freezing cry and heard instead the bawl of the lead steer smelling water from afar. His nostrils tightened to the shrink of the frost in its bitter breath and smelled in its place only the sweet dust and pungent manure of the southern bedding grounds in spring.

Ben Allison was already in Fort Worth, gathering his men and grading his cattle.

Not so the towering Clint.

The younger brother shouldered his sorrel into Ben's black.

"I know what you're thinkin', bud," he said evenly. "Count me out. It's plumb crazy. First off, it cain't be did. Next off, we've nothin' but this bastard's word that he won't turn us in the minute he gits the chance. Last off, the money's ourn, he ain't offerin' us nothin'. Not a damn solitary thing," he let the words drop like cold water on a flat rock, "savin' a certain dose of hemp fever served up atop a kicked-out whiskey barrel."

"That, for sure," nodded Ben. "Against the long odds of bein' suthin' we ain't had no other chance to be—nor ain't likely to git no other chance to be."

"Sech as honest men, I suppose!" rasped Clint sarcastically.

"Sech as honest men," said Ben simply.

Clint's snort of angry derision got stuck halfway out. And stayed there as Nathan Stark calmly spread his full hand.

"I am offering you, *each of you*," he stressed softly, "one third of the chips in a game that could make the biggest raise any man ever played a royal flush to. More money, and *honest* money, than you could whore-up in six lifetimes. Against that," he concluded deliberately, "you are gambling a few thousand dollars in your pocket, the spending of which, ten-to-one, will wind you up in some state's prison for the rest of your useless life."

The prospect had been purposely put in terms Clint understood. And so well put as to slow even his wild mind. But that mind, once slowed, was still as devious and quick as Ben's was straight forward and slow. It slashed now, like a wolf, at what appeared the vulnerable hock tendon of Stark's offer.

"And what's to keep us," he sneered, "that is, providin' we would admire to be honest men like my weakminded partner, here, suggests, from simply usin' yer money to run our own herd up from Texas?"

"Two things," said Stark quietly. "Me and the Sioux Nation."

"Well, now," drawled Clint, beginning in his perverse way to enjoy the debate, "you don't bother me none whatsoever. But what's this here about the Sioux Nation?"

"You've got to cross it to get to the Gallatin."

"So, we cross it."

"Not quite. The Army's got it closed to through civilian travel. There's one trail across it and that's the Bozeman Road. Nobody gets up the Bozeman without a military permit and troop escort."

"Fair enough," shrugged Clint. "We git a military permit and troop escort."

"Precisely the point, my thickheaded friend. *You* don't."

"It's a deal. We don't. Where's that leave you?"

"I *do*," said Nathan Stark.

"Talk don't sell no higher in Montana than it does in

Texas, Mr. Stark." It was Ben, plodding back into the conversation. "How do we know you do?"

"You said you would listen to a man as long as he made sense. Listen to this—both ears.

"I've been freighting for the Union Army since Fort Sumter. The whole five years of that time from Leavenworth to Virginia City, *up the Bozeman*. I can get anything I want cleared beyond Fort Laramie. And two troops of cavalry to see that it stays cleared."

It was enough of a mouthful to make even Clint chew a minute before he spit it out. While he was chewing, Ben swallowed.

"It's a long way to Texas," he nodded half aloud, "and only ten minutes to Montana."

"Meaning what? asked Clint, holding up on his mouthful.

"Meaning," Nathan Stark answered swiftly for Ben, "that you can be back in the Black Nugget before midnight. And with more money in your poke than twenty men could squander before the spring thaw."

Clint looked uncertainly at Ben.

"We gamble his word against our piece of a three-split chance to make suthin' of ourse'ves," said the latter quietly. Then, still more quietly and laying it finally in front of Clint to raise or call. "It's dealer's choice, *hermano*, with Stark's joker stacked and wild."

"I pass," said Clint, his voice for the one, rare moment as straight as Ben's. But the inevitable, tail-switch grin could not be kept out of it.

"You're still shuckin' 'em, Sam. What do we do?"

Ben looked a long time into the valley below. He hunched the thin fray of his Confederate collar against the building cold in the icy whoop of the wind across the divide. He hefted the moneybelt, not looking at it, nor at Clint, nor at anything. At last he pushed his black up to Stark's Kentucky studhorse, peered, narrow-eyed, for a long three seconds into the expressionless face of its rider.

"We gamble," he said, and handed the moneybelt to Nathan Stark.

Chapter Five

THE THREE RIDERS topped the divide. The horses of the first two, beginning to know the place, slowed their gaits. Their sole reward for the foresight was a twitch of the reins, a soft, southern "Hee-yahh, there. Git along, hoss—"

The knowing mounts responded, moving quickly across the exposed spine of the ridge, as glad perhaps as their riders to be out of the whipcrack of the north wind. The third rider followed them. None of the three looked back. Their figures, bolt upright and big and black, loomed for an instant against the four o'clock skyline, then were swiftly gone.

Thus, on the morning of February 29, 1866, Nathan Stark turned his back on Montana.

Accompanying him were the two Texans remembered by Virginia City only and even then but vaguely, as "Sam Allen" and "Tom Pickett."

It was an ill-assorted trio, scarcely suited by varying natures to travel together, yet destined by history to share a three-thousand mile journey which has no parallel in frontier memory. And to share the perils of that unmapped hegira under the terms of a contract still without peer or counterpart in all the peculiar records of western financial understandings.

In the day and place it was not uncommon to settle matters involving thousands, even millions of dollars with a few words and a firm handshake. The language was simple, the men who used it even simpler. They understood one another. There was no room among them for a man whose word was not the easy equal of his bond, no time among their number for the long talker or the Philadelphia lawyer.

Still and all, the agreement between Nathan Stark and his two Texas confederates was unique.

In the saddlebags of the Virginia Citian's bay stallion reposed $10,000 in Yankee currency. Behind him, in the green-doored vault of Esau Lazarus's Black Nugget stronghouse, was deposited the remaining $30,000 of the Texan's original loot. The name on the deposit slip was Nathan Stark's, and his alone. In the worn jeans of the two cowboys riding ahead of him jingled not a nickel more than jingled

23

there the night of their arrival above Alder Gulch. Yet the Texans were satisfied, the one by personal conviction, the other by fraternal persuasion, that they were equal partners in a corporate if crazy scheme to flood the Gallatin Valley with bawling, longhorn gold. Neither for a minute questioned the legality of their two-thirds claim to the waiting fortune, and only the latter withheld total judgment on the given word of their Virginia City associate.

Unique, indeed, was this western "gentleman's agreement." There had not been even the standard handshake to confirm it!

As has been said, Ben and Clint Allison, the former by slowness, the latter by indifference, were simple men. Just how simple, they had at the moment of their departure from Virginia City no way of knowing. A single fact remained, rock-certain. They had picked the one man in Montana best suited by dangerous combination of brains and ambition to show them.

He had stolen the first pot with his bold raise atop the stage road divide the night of the robbery. He had won the second by convincing his cowboy fellow gamblers that the bulk of their capital must be left behind in his own name, since to bank it with Lazarus under any other would have been certain to arouse curiosity and, ultimately, suspicion of the newcomers. The third and final pot now lay ahead. It would necessarily be a long time in the playing. The cards must be held close, the checks and raises made with the utmost, indirect caution.

As he rode south behind the two men from Lampasas and points west, Nathan Stark had no more doubt of his ability to rake in the last pot than he had shown in taking the first. Simple men had no business drawing cards at his table.

He began the cutthroat process of proving it, at the noon coffee halt.

They had ridden the morning away in silence and slowness, the bitterness of the weather and the force of the prairie-scouring wind saving all talk for the shelter of the noonhalt. Now, resting in the windbreak of a thickly willowed creek-bottom, the scalding coffee working inside them, the drift-wood warmth of the fire, outside them, even the taciturn Ben was ready to pass the time of afternoon.

Sensing the moment, Stark eased into it.

"Boys," he announced casually, "we've got it half made. Only fourteen hundred and eighty-five miles more and we're in business."

24

It was the first time Ben had seen him smile, or heard him speak in other than dead-straight terms. Somehow, to the big Texan's mind, it all at once made him one of them. It took a Westerner to refer to fifteen measly miles, out of fifteen freezing hundred, as half the job already done. And to put back of it a good, dry grin at the same time.

"Well, now, Mr. Stark, I allow you've paced it about right. Leastways, we're on our way."

"And far enough on it," smiled the other, "to drop that 'mister.' I reckon it's time we knew some first names. Real ones, for the best results, I'd say. Mine's Nathan—"

It wasn't a statement, it was a question. Ben knew it.

"You a'ready know ours," he said.

"Do I—?" The smile was still at work, Ben noticed, but maybe straining a little to stay there. Clint didn't miss the effort, either.

"That a question, mister?" he asked flatly.

"Sort it to suit yourselves," shrugged Stark, still slow and friendly. "We'll be calling each other something or other from now till fall. It's a long time to listen to a name you're not used to hearing."

The two Texas riders looked at him a long time, the dying driftwood popping three times before Ben at last nodded. "Mine's Ben Allison," he said quietly. "He's Clint. We're brothers."

Clint's eyes narrowed. He broke his glance from Ben, shifted it to Stark. "Yeah," he breathed softly, "brothers." Then, acidly. "I allow you kin tell which is the big brother. The one with the big mouth."

Ben returned his look, saying nothing. Nathan Stark shrugged easily.

"All right, Ben and Clint, now we know each other. It's the best way, you'll see." He slowed, putting it with patent sincerity. "Any name you give is safe with me, remember that."

Ben nodded. But Clint didn't quite buy it.

"We'll remember it, *Mister Stark*," he said deliberately. "See that you do."

Stark watched him a moment longer.

Under the circumstances only one construction could be put on the younger brother's reply. In the West when a man had been offered your first name, then "mistered" you on purpose, friendship was already out the window. He had been unsure of Clint from the beginning. That unsureness had just been removed. Young Allison's cards were on the table, face

25

up. It was only a question of time before they would have to be called.

With the decision, he turned to Ben, waiting for him to speak. Thoughtfully, the big Texan obliged him.

"I reckon we've a'ready tooken your word, or we wouldn't none of us be here," was all he said. "Let's mosey along. Wind's risin' agin and we got some miles to make 'fore sundown."

Stark nodded, came to his feet, started for the horses. So far, so good. The older brother had used neither the requested "Nathan" nor the rejected "Mister." He was still playing a dumb, open hand. One that could be bet into and built up gradually until all the chips were in the middle of the blanket.

Clint was slower to leave the fire, hanging back to catch Ben.

"You out'n your mind, you crazy bastard? We've knowed this son of a bitch twenty-four hours! And by God for a friendly pat on your dumb butt you've give him information a sheriff couldn't beat out'n you with a gunbarrel in six weeks. What the goddam hell you thinkin' of, Ben?"

"Texas," said Ben. "And three thousand head of San Saba steers. What's yours?"

"A rope," growled Clint. "And a nice handy span of yeller pine rafters."

Ben said nothing, only began to kick the fire into the snow. Clint, starting for his mare, held up. "Now what the hell?" he snapped irritably. "You Injun-jumpy a'ready? For Christ's sake we ain't twenty miles shut of the settlements yet!"

"Never knew the Injun," said Ben softly, "that could count past ten."

For ten straight days they rode south, following the base of the Rockies down past the Three Tetons, crossing below them and over Wind River Pass to come out at Fort Bonneville on the headwaters of the East Fork of the Green River. Tracing the East Fork they hit the main Green, followed it south and east until they struck the old Fort Bridger cutoff on the eighteenth day. Here, Ben wanted to angle east, heading over through the North Park country of Colorado to feel out a trail route for their cattle along the east slope of the main divide. It was the way he and Clint had come north and he wanted Stark to see the good water and grass it made for the whole of the way to the Arkansas, and beyond.

Nathan Stark had other ideas.

No one had ever run a trail down the dry west slope. If they could route one over there, it figured to be freer of Indians and Army alike than any passage east of the mountains.

For eight days they were lost in the arid wilderness of eastern Utah. On the ninth day they cut the valley of a major stream running nearly due east. Ben had had enough of Nathan Stark's leadership. He studied the river and the hazy mountains beyond its eastern vanishing point for a full five minutes, saying nothing. Finally, he looked at Stark.

"This'll be fur enough south. You want to search out your dry-hole route past this water, you'll do it with two other Texans. Me and Clint are swingin' east."

At the headwaters of the stream, three days later, they rode into the fur camp of a Taos fox hunter. The stream, he informed them, was the Eagle Tail River. They were a bare hundred and fifty miles north of the New Mexico line, a shade over the same distance west of Bent's Fort on the Arkansas. It was as much as Ben cared to know, or needed to. He spoke short and he spoke quick, not wanting Stark's opinion and not waiting for it.

"We'll head for Bent's and the short grass," was all he said.

There was no argument from Nathan Stark. By now the Virginia City man was no longer thinking in terms of who was in *real* charge. He swung up and followed Ben and Clint without a word.

Late in the afternoon of the twenty-ninth day from Alder Gulch, they came into the broad valley of the main Arkansas seventy-five miles above Bent's Fort. There was little enough cause for celebration. They had been on the trail a month, had covered little more than two thirds the distance to Fort Worth. And worse, they were out of meat, had no flour and no coffee, had seen no game for three days. Their mounts were nearly used up, were grassbellied and sorefooted, would need at least a week on soft ground and good grain to be fit to travel.

It was agreed a layover had to be figured at Bent's Fort.

The following morning, an unusually clear and warm one for the date, they set off down the Arkansas. The day wore on soft and balmy as only such days can in the perverse spring of southern Colorado. By ten o'clock Ben's and Clint's spirits were considerably uplifted by the continuing brightness of the March sunshine on the homeground of their beloved short-grass country.

The uplift lasted until an hour after noonhalt, when the

sky to the north and east began to lead-up ominously and the wind to whine softly and nervously up the sweeping valley of the Arkansas from the south and east.

Within twenty minutes the grass was lying flat and due southwest and the wind, having switched compass completely, was hammering at them with the unimpeded force of its eight-hundred-mile march across the Kansas and Colorado plains. Seconds later the snow began and the darkness shut down around them blacker than a Montana mine pit.

In the ten-foot lee of a riverbed shelfbank, Ben pulled the black gelding in.

It was two o'clock in the afternoon. A man on horseback could not be seen thirty feet away. It was time for a talk—and in the unprotected sweep of the open prairie a man couldn't hear you if you were yelling in his near ear with a deaf-horn, four inches away and downwind.

"We cain't stop here." He leaned in the saddle, cupping his hands toward Stark. "Got to drift with the river till we hit timber. That's Timpas Crick at Ludlow's Bend this side the fort. 'Nother fifteen, twenty miles mebbe."

The wind caught his words, whipping them across Clint's hunching shoulders, drumming them ominously past the white-faced Stark.

"How far is the fort itself?" he called.

A vicious drive of sleeted snow trapped his question, flung it away from Ben, out across the turgid Arkansas. Clint heard it. *Too far, little man!* he consoled, then handcupped its relay to Ben. "The gentleman from Virginia City rises to request the official distance to Mr. Charley Bent's second-hand store."

"Forty miles, mebbe forty-five," shouted Ben.

Stark waved stiffly, signifying he had heard. "I say we stay right here! We've no chance in this weather!" Nathan Stark had drifted out his share of north plains blizzards, had no stomach for adding this southern specimen to his successful record.

"You say like hell!" bellowed Clint. "This here's a blue Texas norther, mister. Not no Montana chinook. Ain't nobody sets out her dance agin no cutbank. Not and stays spry for the promenade home."

"Clint's right." Ben was shaking out his rope with the shout, flipping its noosed end to Clint. "We got to go on, right now. There's like to be five foot of snow on the level come daylight."

Clint caught the rope, looped it over his mare's head, passing the reins free of it. In the same motion he uncoiled his own rope, shot it, hondo first, toward Stark. The latter caught it, made it fast around his bay's neck. "I hope to God you boys know what you are doing," he shouted to Clint.

Clint laughed, turned his Comanche-dark face to the belly of the blizzard above them.

"*Ka-dih!*" he yelled, calling harshly upon the Southern Comanche's Great Spirit. "You hear the man? Listen to your white brother from Montana, you no-good Injun bastard! Leave off that infernal howlin', you hear?"

"You leave off of it," warned Ben. "It ain't funny to even *play* crazy in a tight like this."

"Brother mine," boomed Clint, his grin flashing white in the darkness, "you been misinformed. *I ain't playin'!*"

"Hang on," ordered Ben. "We're goin' out."

With the wave, he kicked the black gelding out past the cutbank. Behind him the thirty-foot lengths of the Texas lariats sang tight. The three-horse chain cleared the bank, the weary mounts staggering as the full blast of the hurricane wind struck them. They were lost to view in as many seconds as they had men in their saddles, and in as many more the ironshod marks of their passing were flattened and filled with the white smother of the driving snow.

In the center of a south plains blizzard all senses are at once destroyed. A man is a blind, deaf mute, his mount an unreasoning, terror stricken wild animal, fighting both him and the storm with equal dumb-brute fury. All points of the prairie compass are blotted out. In any direction and in all directions the fearful needle may swing, only blackness beckons, only death by cold awaits. There is no time, nor any sense of it. A minute may be an hour, an hour but twenty seconds—or five—or no seconds at all.

Fighting for his breath against the strangling clot of the snow, Ben kept the black moving. Behind him Clint's and Stark's horses fought the growing drifts. He could see neither of them, hear nothing but the insane yammer of the wind. He knew they were there only by the tension on his rope.

How long they had been riding before he realized they had lost the river, he did not know. He only knew that one minute the yellow surge of the Arkansas was still roiling ten feet to his left, and then there was nothing over there where it should be but the piling, dirty white of the unbroken snows.

He did not stop the black and did not dare to.

There was no chance for them, now, which they would not

make worse by a rope-tangling halt. He kept the black digging, reining him back to the left, cursing him on.

The big horse fought him at once. He threw his head, flinging and jawing at the bar of the bit, bowing his neck, humping his spine, grunting and whickering fiercely. Ben put the spurs into him to their shanks, nearly jerked his head off sawing back on the left rein. The horse took it and held now to the left, but a man could feel by the way he went, sidestepping and hipswinging constantly to the right, that he was being driven against his crazed will.

Ben began to count now, shouting the numbers aloud. That river had to be close, he could not have lost it more than a few seconds. But time was a crazy thing when a man could not see or hear. If he lost track of it now—

The count reached one hundred. Then two. The leaden pile of the snow rolled on, unbroken. At two hundred and fifty, Ben knew five minutes had gone. And that the Arkansas had gone with them.

All that was left now was something he had been told all the days of his ranch boyhood was no good—a horse's sense of direction in a blue norther. But in the big Texan's mind was another memory from that same boyhood, and not from the ranch. A memory from that other part of that boyhood. One from the Comanche camps along the North Concho. The red brother did not agree with the white. There was a proverb among those Kwahadis. An old, old proverb. From a people who had been horse Indians a hundred years before the Sioux left Minnesota on foot, or the broadfaced Cheyenne trudged down onto the plains from their Uinta Mountain fastnesses. A proverb that went, *"Tsei hou-dei kyh-gou-p gaux-kin*—a blind horse has more brains than a bright man in a blizzard!"

Ben eased up on the black, shook out the reins, let them fall slack. The horse stopped dead. He gathered his haunches, stood waiting uncertainly. Ben shook the reins again, ticked him with the spurs, leaned up in the saddle.

"Go along, you black bastard!" he yelled. "I ain't bright and you ain't blind, but we're sure as hell in a blizzard!"

The big gelding flung his head around, walled his eyes at his crouching rider. He blew the snow from the moist red bell of his nostrils, began shortly to move ahead. Within twenty steps Ben felt him veer back to the right. Before a minute had passed, he had completely reversed their left-hand course, was blundering and bucking the hock-deep.

snows in a direction Ben's instincts told him was directly away from the river.

"*Ka-dih!*" Ben yelled into the storm, suddenly thinking of Clint and his crazy laugh. "Don't you make no liar out'n me and my poor old grandmother!"

Hearing the shout, the black seemed to redouble both the speed and sureness of his stride. Ben let him go. He was feeling the cold now. Feeling its tingling, swift deadliness closing in on him. Numbing its spreading way up his arms and legs. Creeping relentlessly past wrist and ankle. Pushing its leaden weight toward knee and elbow.

As it did, he knew without benefit of white boyhood ranch lore or red-memoried Kwahadi proverb exactly where the black gelding was taking him and Clint and Nathan Stark. Once you knew that, the next grim question for Ka-dih was easy.

How long did it take three white men to freeze to death in the belly of a blue Texas norther?

Chapter Six

THERE WAS NO WAY for a man to know how long he had been unconscious in the saddle. He only knew something struck him heavily along the right thigh, then twice along the left, nearly scraping him from his horse. He remembered pawing for the saddlehorn, getting his eyes open. Then he saw them, thick and blackstemmed, all around him.

Trees. Cottonwoods, alders, willows. They were in the timber. Dense, grove-thick timber. Timber that shut out the hammer of the wind as suddenly as though there had never been a blizzard.

They were saved. Saved by the grace of Ka-dih and the memory of a Comanche proverb—by the will of a heathen Kwahadi god and the brains of a "blind," black horse.

The big gelding had brought them into Timpas Creek Grove.

It was only seconds after Ben's clearing vision recorded the trees that he was aware of the fire which gleamed beyond them. Moments later, the black broke free of the intervening scrub and into the tiny cleared space which sheltered the blaze.

The snow blindness was still harsh and glaring in front of his peering eyes. Ben could make out only blurred forms coming toward him. His ears, still full of the shriek and howl of the outer wind, could not clearly distinguish the voices which came with the forms.

He tried to dismount, to get down off the black gelding and move to meet them. He could not. His frozen limbs would not relinquish their hold of the horse's barrel.

He remembered the voices growing suddenly clear and close, saw for a moment the swim of upturned, white faces which came with them. He felt, numbly and far off, the reach and grasp of the friendly hands. Then the momentary clearness withdrew. The faces faded out, the voices fell away. There was an instant's prolonged sensation, half floating, half falling, of leaving the saddle and coming away from the black gelding. After that, there was nothing but the darkness and the silence.

His next memory was so disturbingly beautiful he wondered for an idle, suspended moment if despite a hard and heretic life he had not somehow managed to get past the pearly gate check point. To slip by old St. Pete, unculled, and make it on into the celestial range with the main herd of highgrade beef.

But at that precise moment the surpassingly lovely vision chose to smile down upon him. With that smile all thoughts of the great beyond faded from Ben Allison's mind. There would be no place in heaven for a smile like that, nor for the face that smile was coming out of. Only the devil could fashion a set of lips like those. And hell alone could hold the haunting beauty of the face behind their moist, warm curve.

"Easy now, partner. Feeling better—?"

He could only nod, dumb and stiff, and go on looking up at that face.

It was an oval, angular face, carved that way by nature to begin with and now hollowed and wasted to a shadowed gauntness that told at a glance of the hunger and privation which inhabited the little camp they had stumbled upon. The drawn skin was startlingly white save for where the wide, red fullness of the warm mouth broke its pallor. The eyes, set deep and wide above the sculptured cheekbones, were of a dark cobalt, almost an indigo blue. And at their outer corners they had that sweeping upslant which put their long lashes to curving black and wicked above their depthless color.

"Don't strain yourself, stranger." The voice was as deep and disturbing as the eyes. "You're not strong enough to be thinking about *that* yet."

If Ben was a simple man, he was not that simple. Her boldness hit him hard and bad, and he did not like it. "I'm sorry, ma'am," he muttered. "Guess I'm purty done in. Didn't mean to stare, I reckon."

"Reckon none of you ever gets too done in to take a good look," said the girl evenly. Then, the full lips breaking away to show the snowflash of the teeth again, "Coffee's on and long boiled. I'll get you a tin."

The way she put it let a man know she was from his own country, at least from somewhere west of the Big Muddy and not any eastern or northern girl. And the tone and look she put behind it let him know he wasn't the first hombre that had sidled up to her and been eared down for his trouble.

In the moment before she returned he found himself already wondering about her, who she was and where she had come from. The same moment was long enough to tell him that while she may have come with these people, she was not one of them. The rest of the folks in the little camp were em-

33

igrants, pure and simple. Sod hut farmers, for sure. Looking to be from the Missouri or more likely the Kaw bottomlands from say around Olathe or Fort Leavenworth. And heading west chasing the same old settler shadow—more and better land and fewer folks to share it with.

A man could see all that in the one glance he had time to throw across the fire to where they were fussing with Clint and Stark.

There were just seven of them, all told. Four men, three women, not counting the girl. Naturally, she made eight. But she didn't belong and you counted her out, right off. The others were all older people, tired and gray looking, without children or the hope of children, and mean poor. Their three slatbed wagons and half-dozen ribsprung mules weren't fit for a Sunday drive around the settlements, let alone for bucking out across the open prairies to God knew where.

But by the time you got to that point, the girl was back with your coffee and you were thinking about nothing else but getting it past your frost-cracked lips and down into your solid-ice belly.

After it was down there you'd have a better head for asking questions.

Ben seized the steaming tin, not feeling the sear of it on his numbed fingers. He fumbled it, almost dropping it, and the girl took it away from him.

"I'll pour, you drink," she ordered softly.

Before he could move to object, she had an arm behind him and the cup to his lips, was pressing that close to him that no amount of snow and cold could keep the fragrant, heated perfume of her body away.

"Damn it all, ma'am, I kin feed my ownse'f—!"

He straightened awkwardly, shouldering her away, reaching for the coffee tin. She shrugged, laughed, low and bubbly like slowing mountain water, handed him the tin. "Don't be bashful, boy," she murmured. "I won't bite. At least," she paused, eying him, "not till you're better."

He took the coffee, needing both hands to get it to his mouth. When it was drained, he handed the tin back, caught her level stare and held it. "All right, ma'am, let's have it. Who're these folks and what're you all doin' here?"

"Back where I come from," said the girl, "strangers don't ask questions."

"Back where I come from," echoed Ben slowly, "strangers don't ask questions less'n they're aimin' to git answers."

"So what?"

"So I got a big nose for trouble, girl—" She didn't miss the omission of the previous "ma'am," nonetheless gave no sign of it, sat waiting through the little pause ahead of his conclusion. "Right now," Ben grunted, "I'm smellin' bad news, back to back, hunkered tight down on this camp."

The girl looked at him, nodding slowly.

"There's nothing wrong with your nose, mister. We've got hard luck till hell won't have it. Question still is," she added expressionlessly, "so what?"

Ben returned the look, feeling the hardness of the girl and the bitter strength of her. "So nothin', ma'am." His own face was without expression now. "We owe you and your folks one, that's all."

"Meaning what?"

"Meanin' we aim to pay off, likely."

"With what?" she shrugged caustically.

Ben saw how it was with her, then. Three shrunken-bellied men, unfed and provisionless, had stumbled into a winter-bound camp where there wasn't enough food for the eight souls already starving to death in it. He found the girl's eyes again, his voice softening.

"That bad?" he said quietly.

"That bad," she nodded. "The coffee you just had was *it*."

"No fatback? No beans?"

"No saltpork for three weeks. Beans gave out three days ago. There was a little parched corn for the mules. We boiled it day before yesterday. Last of it went last night." She stopped, then nodded with a sudden, strangely bright smile. "I've been eying that damn lead mule all day!"

Ben nodded, came stiffly to his feet.

"Well, keep eying him," he said, wide mouth spreading to the first of the quick grins. "And learn yourse'f suthin." He fumbled the cavalry coat open, slid out from its hidden neck-thonged sheath the eight-inch blade of the Kwahadi skinning knife.

"Up-comin', ma'am, you got one damn fast, free and first-hand lesson on how they dress out Missouri Elk along the bonnie Arkansas—"

The girl rose lithely, stood facing him, her upturned face white against the storm darkness pressing in on the fire's thin glow. The taunting, cynical smile was swiftly gone from the parted lips, their full warmth framing itself heatedly behind the low words. "You speak my language, mister. *My name's Nella Torneau.*"

It was a whisper meant just for him, coming deliberately

back-turned to the fire and to the others beyond its light. Ben checked to its soft challenge, stood towering over her, silent now and suddenly narrow-eyed.

"Mine's Ben Allison," he said at last. "Likely we'll git on, you and me."

He wheeled away with the words, all at once awkward and angry with having said them, and with the way he had said them. He strode quickly toward the picketline, not looking back, not wanting to look back. He had said enough already. It was time to get away from her, far away from her, before he said too much. Women like that were not for him. He had little way with the best of them, none whatever with her kind.

The girl watched him until his lean form was only a shadow, lost beyond the picketline and the nightfall gloom of the eddying snow gusts. When she moved at last toward the fire and the huddled group around it, the haunting half curve of the wanton smile was back in cynical place.

Ben Allison had not turned away quickly enough.

He had already said too much.

Clint and Stark, recovering from their ordeal more slowly than Ben, did not see Nella Torneau until she returned to the fire after watching the latter start for the picketed mules. At this late point Clint had only time to stumble to his feet and breathe his standard, "Good Gawd Amighty!" when Ben was calling over to him to come help with the butchering.

Turning to go, Clint took another long look at the girl, noting a few things his less worldly brother had not. Like the winter-pelt glossiness of her hair. And how blue-black and luxuriant as any Indian woman's it was beneath the fox fur hood of her parka. But also how deep-curly and soft it was, like no Indian woman's that ever lived. Then, too, the full, long grace of her figure, hardly complimented by the formless bulk of the old wolfskin trapper's coat she had wrapped around it. Still, to an eye as young in ideas and old in practice as Clint's, no set of pelts could hide the thrust of those deep breasts, nor the wicked mold and movement of those curving buttocks. Then, lastly, it wasn't just having those things under that coat, but the way she stared back at you when she caught you noticing them that told you she was not only all the woman she looked, but more than likely not too dead set against proving it to you.

Ben, whether noting his hesitation and its reason or merely anxious to get on with the skinning-out, called again and irritably now, and Clint grinned. To Nathan Stark, gaping open-mouthed at the girl as though he had never seen a set of breasts before—not even under a winter coat—he drawled broadly. "Lay off. You hear me, little man? I seen 'em first."

He said it deliberately loud, so that the girl would not miss it.

She didn't.

"Run along, junior," she said unsmilingly. "Go help daddy cut up the nice mule. Mother's hungry."

Clint laughed.

He threw back his head and really let it come out in that sudden crazy way of his. Then, just as quickly, his voice was back in its old appealing drawl. "Mama," he grinned loosely, "you ain't one half so hungry as little Clinton Allison! Age, twenty-three, ma'am," he said soberly. "Free, three quarters white, and single as a skunk at a Sunday school picnic."

With that and a second quick laugh, he was gone, striding free and long across the snow toward the picketline, whistling and swinging his wide shoulders as though starvation, south plains blizzards and slaughtering mules were all in the average day's work.

Nella looked after him as she had Ben before him, but with one difference.

For Clint there was no curving smile. there was only the trace of tightness around the long-lashed eyes, the hint of uneasiness in the straightened set of the soft lips. This one would make trouble. All women were alike to his kind. You could see his play coming a mile across the table, and you knew there was no least chance of bluffing him out of it.

She shrugged, turning her cool stare on the last man.

Nathan Stark blushed, lowered his eyes, got suddenly busy with his empty coffee cup.

"It's all gone, mister," she said to him sarcastically. "You can suck on that tin till spring and you won't get another drop."

This third stranger was not her kind. Maybe he was big and maybe he was all the man he looked. But he was too square and heavy through the body, too dully straight and blankfaced as well, and too dead set and bulldoggy looking around the jaw. That kind got ahold of a woman and never let her go. And never gave themselves, or her, an inch of love or fun in the bargain.

With the dismissal she turned away from him to the emigrant menfolk of her own party. Rousing them from the apathetic regard of the fire, into which they had sunk back following the resuscitation of the frozen newcomers, she began rattling orders with all the feminine delicacy of an outpost drill sergeant.

"You, Jed Bates, leave off your mooning and stir up the fire. Tom, you haven't had any tobacco in that pipe for three days. Now quit sucking on it like a damn lost calf and get out and rustle in some more wood. Mr. Johnson, you chop up what he lugs in. Todd Bliss, rig up a spit. Best make a rack for the pot, too. Miz Bates—!" She called toward the wagons, one of the grayfaced women peering out beneath the canvas in dull-eyed answer. "Bring the big kettle. Scoop it full of snow on your way. The boys are killing a mule. We'll boil a mess for tomorrow the same time we're roasting that for tonight.

"You, stranger—" She turned on Stark, her short words giving no lie to the dislike of him already forming in her. "Get off your dead end and go help Tom tote in some limbs. Don't strain your milk now. Let him heft the heavy ones."

Fascinated, Nathan Stark followed Tom out into the trees. He could not get his eyes or his mind off the strange, tall girl who talked like a logging camp bully, yet moved about with a sinuous, she-wolf voluptuousness more wantonly female than any woman he had ever seen.

Long after Ben and Clint had lost themselves in the blood and sweating blasphemy of the mule butchering, and Nella Torneau had forgotten him in the work of preparing the fireside against the rewards of that butchering, his eyes continued to follow the girl. He had never been this close to her kind before, nor in fact close to any woman before. Nathan Stark was twenty-eight and had never had a woman of any kind. There had been no time for one in his grubbing, heavy-handed quest to make of himself a rich and powerful man.

Now, suddenly, he wanted Nella Torneau more than all the gold in Alder Gulch—or as close as he could come to wanting *anything* more than gold.

And he decided as quickly, and in his blunt-jawed, inexorable way, that he would have her. Peculiar to that willful, blind way, and to his seeing in it only the purposes and ends of his own insatiable hunger for self and success, the decision itself was tantamount to possession.

The girl *was* his.

No one else should ever have her.

Chapter Seven

THE RAVENOUS DISAPPEARANCE of the first fifteen pounds of half-roasted mule tenderloin, plus a stout, bitter brew of willowbark tea concocted by the wilderness-wise Ben, brought the lowered spirits of the starving emigrant party back to the halfmast of rearoused hope. The presence of the two tall Texans, both clearly born to and masters of the heartless country surrounding them, worked an additional palliative of its own. Confidence and good humor alike returned, and within the hour the full story of the camp's desperate plight was out.

They were Kansans, as Ben had suspected. Their goal had been Oregon but owing to the risk of late winter storms inherent in the calculated gamble of a February start from the settlements, they had taken the southern route of the Smokey Hill Stageline. They had planned to leave it and turn north along the Rockies, hoping an early spring would catch up with them en route. Nella Torneau had joined them at the last stage station on the Smokey Hill run, before that road turned south. She had left the stage for reasons of her own, neither asked nor offered. She had simply sought and paid well for passage north. And she had proved the sole stroke of good fortune encountered on the journey. There was no mistaking the sober respect with which the emigrant men acknowledged the fact, nor the grateful nods with which their womenfolk agreed to it.

But the luck of Nella Torneau was not enough.

The expected spring weather failed to match miles with their weary progress. The feared late winter storms closed the Denver and old Fort St. Vrain wagonroads, driving them back south and forcing them to seek refuge at the nearest known outpost—Bent's Fort on the Arkansas. They had missed the Bent's trail somewhere south of the Smokey Hill road, had wound up four days ago at Ludlow's Bend and Timpas Creek.

To Ben's mind, the story left but one clear course: get the party back into its wagons, guide them on into the fort as soon as the snow melted off. There was plenty of mulemeat and no question of anybody going hungry short of that meltoff.

Nathan Stark at once objected.

"We've got to get on, Ben," he insisted with patent serious-ness. "Why, it may be days after the weather breaks before the snow goes out to where wagons and weak mules can get through."

"No matter," said Ben flatly. "We ain't leavin' these folks."

"Nothing," added Clint, eying Nella, "could persuade us to such purfidjous ideas."

"Don't be damn fools," said Stark angrily. "I'm not sug-gesting we abandon these people. We can send a pack outfit to bring them in. They can be safe in the fort twenty-four hours after we get there."

There was no denying that, and Ben knew it. Knew, too, that he would have thought of it himself had his mind not been so full of that slinky girl. "It figgers," he admitted. "We'll head out soon's the snow lets up."

"Which won't be long," added Nathan Stark tersely.

Ben caught his glance, followed it up through the naked blackness of the willow and cottonwood branches.

The twisted limbs still bent and writhed to the wind's lash-ing violence. But beyond their tortured web, above the thin-ning drive of the snow, high and clear and black over the brooding stillness of Timpas Creek Grove, a narrow window of clean sky opened briefly.

The angry wind gathered in a bellyful of flying snow and instantly and howlingly slammed that window shut. But Ben had seen the distant, light-quick dance of the stars. Stark was right. The blizzard had blown its guts out, would bleed itself to death sometime during the night.

"We'll go with first light," he said to Clint and Nathan Stark. Then, turning to the waiting, hopeful members of the little emigrant band, he nodded softly. "Folks, you kin turn in and sleep easy. The wind's about done. Come mornin' she'll be bell clear and lamb quiet, fur as you kin see up or down the Arkansaw. We'll make the fort 'fore noon. Your troubles will be plumb past, come sundown tomorrow night."

With the reassurance, the camp was soon asleep, the emi-grants in their covered slatbed wagons, Ben and his compan-ions rolled in their blankets by the fire. The minds of the former were at rest with the clearing weather and Ben's guar-antee of their troubles being over by nightfall of the follow-ing day.

Their sleep might well have been less sound had they known how eternally right was the tall Texan's prediction. For the troubles of the gauntfaced Kansas pilgrims would indeed be over with sundown of the next day—and over for all the sundowns that would ever follow.

The buffalo skull is the signpost of the prairie.

Upon it the prowling wolf and the skulking coyote void their spattered stain, leaving yellowed word of warning to their next of passing kin that the territory is already pre-empted. Trotting sorefooted in their wake, the sad-eared settlement hound hangs back behind the dust of the last wagon to scar the prairie sod with stiff thrusted scratches of his hind feet and to void, in disdainful turn, his leg-hoisted contempt of the wild brother's warning. The twelve-year-old boy, out-riding the head of the next train with his watchful father, tarries a moment to dig in homespun trousers' pocket for precious bit of charcoal, and to scrawl upon the whitened bone his own small footnote to a larger history.

Lastly, there are others of the wasteland's wanderers to whom the whited skull is both signpost and signal station. It was of these last two-footed nomads Ben Allison was thinking as he sat his lathered black ten miles east of Timpas Creek Grove.

"What you think, Clint?" He broke his eyes from the buffalo skull with the question, sweeping the empty stillnesses of the valley, east and west.

Clint studied the skull. About it were the freshly manured tracks of many unshod ponies. From around it to the level of the brown earth upon which it rested, the burying snows had been carefully banked and pushed back. Above the right eye socket a crude human hand, palm down and fingers pointing to the ground, had been daubed in gaudy vermilion. Above the left eye, starkly drawn in black charcoal grease-paste, was a Sharps buffalo rifle, the barrel broken away from the stock at the point of the breech, and pointing abruptly earthward. Below the eye sockets, across the bridge of the foreface, was what appeared to be two human ears connected by a straight, slashing line in garish ocher yellow.

Clint shook his head. There was no grin lighting his handsome features, no customary easy softness in his tightlipped drawl. "By Gawd, I dunno, Ben. The hand and the busted gun read clear enough. They couldn't mean but one thing, no matter the tribe that drawed them. But son of a bitch if I kin figger the yeller scrawl."

"Nor me," said Ben. "But likely we'd better figger it. It's their road brand, that's certain. Jest as certain, we'd best know what herd they're cut out'n."

"Well, I kin tell you two things," nodded Clint. "It ain't from no Kiowa nor no Comanche herd."

"Thanks," said Ben, "for nothin'." Then, quickly. "Git Stark over here. He jest might know."

"Now mebbe he jest might," Clint agreed. "I allow it's about time he knowed suthin'. Fer a man that's so big in Montana he's sure been gradin' short yearlin' south of his home range."

"Give him time," advised Ben. "He's four-year-old beef. Jest new to the trail, I judge. Git him over here."

Clint grunted something Ben didn't hear, but that sounded as if it had son of a bitch and Montana mixed up in it somewhere, and spurred his mare on back to where Stark waited in the main trail.

"Twist your two-bit tail," he called cheerfully. "We need a educated man up here that kin read summat besides Kiowa and Comanche billy-doos."

Stark took one look at the pictograph on the bull's skull, lost a layer or two of his fresh pink color, used a single agonized word both to justify Ben's faith in his Indian higher learning and to let the Texas brothers know upon whose tribal crossroads they were trespassing.

"*Sioux—!*" he gasped unbelievingly.

"The hell!" challenged Clint, not caring for the startled diagnosis. "I thought this here Arkansaw basin was Cheyenne country."

"It is," said Nathan Stark. "From the river, north to Fort Laramie and the Oregon Road. But that signature is Oglala Sioux."

"You certain sure?" asked Ben.

"No chance I'm wrong. I've not studied their signs much, never had to in my business. But I do know that yellow symbol. Saw it splashed on the tailgate of a wagon burn-out up on the Bozeman last summer. I had one of Colonel Carrington's Army scouts with me, and he read it off for us. That long slash connecting what look like ears, there, is a knife cut. That's what the Oglala call themselves—the Throat Cutters."

He broke off, frowning at the bright red hand and broken gun as Ben and Clint exchanged looks, then added, puzzled. "What does the rest of it mean?"

"The hand," recited Clint with mile-wide irony, and as though reading it for him from the prairie primer on the facts of life in the far West, "if drawn upright with the fingers pointing to the sky and the palm outward, means peace.

The gun, if in one piece and also aiming at the great blue beyond, indicates the selfsame Christian intention."

Stark was looking to Ben, as he had from the outset, hearing Clint's hardbitten recital but waiting for the older brother's less caustic seal of acceptance.

He was not kept waiting overlong.

"The rest of it," repeated Ben Allison slowly, *"means war."*

The discussion grew swiftly bitter.

"I don't give a damn what you say," rapped Nathan Stark. "Our best bet is to go on to the fort. Those pony tracks are heading west. Our course is east."

"My course is where I say it is," said Ben. "And I say it's back to that emigrant camp."

"Ben, be reasonable," pleaded Stark, placing a friendly hand on his shoulder. "There's only ten or twelve of the Indians. They've nothing to gain by attacking those poor devils back there. It doesn't make sense."

"Don't it?" smiled Clint easily. "Take a look at that north sky, mister."

Stark glanced nervously at the greasy mushroom bed of clouds growing rapidly beyond the river, then defiantly back to Clint. "All right. The clouds are coming in heavy again. Where's the difference? We can beat them to the fort."

"The Sioux," nodded Ben, pale eyes narrowing, "kin likewise beat 'em to the grove."

"I don't follow you, Ben."

"Well, follow this!" Clint shoved his mare into Stark's studhorse. "You said you didn't know much about Injuns. Mister, you don't. They ain't partial to snowstorms no more'n white men. It's damn seldom how few times you'll bump up agin a war party out joggin' a blizzard jest fer the fresh air. Also, they got bellies jest like us. They git hungry and they got to eat. You know how much game we've seen the past week. You kin lay they ain't seen no more where they come from. It jest ain't the weather fer game. She all adds up, mister."

"To what, for God's sake?" demanded Nathan Stark angrily.

"To Timpas Creek Grove and them five emigrant mules," said Ben quietly. "I reckon we got to go back."

"Yeah," muttered Clint, reining the mare sharply. "And sometime 'fore spring would be nice."

"Well, you reckon wrong," declared Stark, still angry. "And without me. I've got ten thousand dollars in these sad-

43

dlebags and it's going to get to Fort Worth, emigrant mules or no emigrant mules."

"What about emigrant jennies?" said Clint innocently, letting his slack grin loosen with the question.

Stark knew he meant the girl, and *what* he meant about the girl. But he covered his hand. "I won't waste words with an idiot," he snapped loftily. Then, wheeling his stud to face Ben, flatteringly, "Ben, you're a man that makes sense, and understands it as well. I'm appealing to you now. Use that sense, man. Think! Why, we can—"

"You're bellerin' inter the wind," muttered Ben. He kicked his gelding around. "You comin', Clint?"

Clint held the little sorrel in, making no move to send her after the black. "Not jest yet," he said, hardfaced.

"You stickin' with Stark, Clint?"

The straight-eyed, too soft way Ben said it let Clint know his refusal had caught his brother like a knife in the kidney. But his own face lost no line of its hardness.

"Stark," he answered, just as low, *"and our ten thousand dollars."*

It was the difference in them, that Ben had made nothing of Stark's mention of the money. But Clint's reminder of it was something else again. Something even Ben couldn't miss, nor ignore, nor even blame.

"Likely, you've got a good point. Leastways," he shrugged, "the way you see it."

There was no bitterness in the words. Clint knew none was intended. Ben was like that. Still a man knew what store his brother set by certain things. Knew, in that line, that ten times ten thousand dollars could not have kept Ben from going back to help those poor bastards on Timpas Creek.

"We'll git to the fort and back quick as we kin," he muttered awkwardly. Then, harshly, to Stark, "Kick that studhorse in his blue-blooded butt, mister. We got miles to make."

Ben watched them go. He heeled the black gelding once more and finally around.

With the slap of the reins, the right spur raked the black's side, leaping him into an ears-flat gallop. Behind him, as he raced the narrow trackline of the Sioux war ponies, came the first of the returning blizzard's sleeted forebreath. Crouched atop him, Ben was thinking they had some miles to make, too. And knowing they wouldn't make their miles on *blue* blood, but red!

Chapter Eight

THE RISING WIND was behind Ben, whipping out of the north-east, driving hard past him, full toward the grove. He did not hear the firing until he was breaking clear of Ludlow's Bend, almost atop the Timpas Creek timber. He had had sense enough to drop the black down below the river bluffs as he approached the camp. It was all that saved him from riding right up the rumps of the Sioux ponies.

With the flat, wind-buffeted report of the first rifle shot, he was off the big horse like a cat.

Ka-dih must still have been watching over his quarter-bred grandson for he had placed in the precise spot where Ben slid the black to a halt a heavy stand of riverbank willows. Tying the horse, and not worrying about him winding the Indian ponies, since the near gale force of the wind was dead away from the willows, he ran crouching forward to the edge of the leafless thicket.

The first look was all a man needed to show him he had bitten off a Texas-sized mouthful.

Up the streambed perhaps a hundred yards, directly opposite the grove and not over fifty paces from it, the hostiles were bedded in against the river bank. They had a clear field of fire into the little camp, impeded only by the outer fringe of trees and the hastily barricaded slatbed wagons. The return fire from the grove could only serve to prevent a frontal charge, since the red attackers were quite comfortable behind five solid feet of yellow Arkansas bank clay. The hostiles, never in their conception of prairie warfare willing to accept casualties for no reason, could afford to take their time.

They were taking it.

There were nine of them, Ben counted; all dressed in the knee length, buffalo hide boots and wolfskin coats which were the standard Plains Indian winter garb. They were bare-headed, of course, some wearing copper braid ornaments, some only an eagle feather or two. Five of them had muzzle-loading trade muskets, the other four, only war bows or short buffalo lances. From the stark lack of feathers or other foo-fooraw in their attire, a man drew one quick conclusion. These boys were in business. They were not out to make social conquests.

Ben, accustomed as he was to the short, broadbodied physiques of the southern tribes, was at once struck with the size of the northern nomads. He had heard the Sioux were a tall people, but not *how* tall. There wasn't a buck up that riverbed that would go half a hand under six feet, and several of them towered well over the two-yard mark.

Recovering from the first unpleasantness of having ridden, but for the sake of a lucky bend in the river, into this nest of six-foot red hornets, Ben's eyes suddenly narrowed.

In the huddle of the Sioux ponies, standing rumps-to-wind beyond their darkfaced masters, he now counted ten mounts. With the belated correction, his scalp squeezed in and his hand tightened on the breech of his Henry carbine.

Somewhere out yonder, or maybe handclose in the willows around him, he had a missing Indian.

The thought had only formed, when he found him.

Upstream, beyond the entrenched Sioux, the left bank of the Arkansas built into a considerable bluff. Atop this prominence, silhouetted against the sleeting gray of the winter sky, stood the tenth Indian.

Unless the distance fooled you, he was not as tall as the others. He was dressed in black wolfskins from head to foot, with the scarlet slash of a Three Point Hudson's Bay blanket shrouding his narrow shoulders and trailing to the snows behind him. And, by God, unless you didn't know as much about Plains Indians as you thought you did—which right now wasn't half as much as you *wished* you did—what he was doing up there, was praying!

But there could be no misreading the ramrod stiffness of his posture, nor the stock-still, outstretched appeal of the suppliant arms. To Ben, suddenly, there was something sinister about that Indian. Something about his black furs and his rail-thin motionlessness that got into a man like the other nine put together hadn't done.

He shrugged off the chill, blaming the cut of the north wind for it. At least there was one thing damn certain about that religious redskin. If he was praying, it wasn't for peace. When an Indian did that, his gun was always placed on the ground in front of him. In the upraised hands of this black-robed brother reposed a Henry Repeating Rifle as short and sweet and ugly as the one now getting sweated in his own shrinking grasp.

Well, no matter. Nine working at war and one praying for it, or not. A man knew what he had to do. And what he had to do was get through them and into that emigrant camp.

He had seven shots in the Henry. If he couldn't get five of

those bucks with that seven rounds, at that peashooter range of not over a hundred yards, he was in the wrong business. Naturally, after that, the ball was over and the band could go home. The rest of them would be falling in on him like a rotten roof, and a man would have to figure his chances lay somewhere between how fast he could get back to the black and how slow the Sioux could scramble for their ponies. There wasn't any use trying to guess it past there. He would only get the shakes and spoil his aim.

Ben got on his belly, moved his elbows around in the snow until he found firm ground under both of them. He wedged himself down solid, cheeked the Henry, lined up the first buck and squeezed off.

It was a head shot. The Indian never moved. He just buckled a little in the knees, eased gently forward into the bank, was out of the fight for keeps. He got two others through the body in as many seconds, then his luck and their surprise ran out together.

A freakish gust of wind boiled up the groundsnow between him and his running targets, obscuring the Sioux for a full five seconds. In that time they had made it to their ponies and were vaulting up on them. The air was still dancing with blown snow as he levered the last four shots into them.

A man feels things with his rifle. If he *knows* it. Ben knew that Henry from bent foresight to battered buttplate. He was just as sure his past four shots were wasted as he was certain his first three were center-ring, meat-in-the-pot, solid.

Going for the black, he shifted the empty carbine to his left hand, whipped out the Kwahadi knife with his right. It was too long after lunch to be fussing with tied reins. He went aboard the gelding like a charging grizzly swarming over a crippled buffalo heifer. The Kwahadi blade slashed, the San Saba "Hee-yahhh!" echoed hoarsely, and the race was on.

For the first forty jumps he guided the black with his knees, using his hands for a few other things that needed to be done before spring set in. Like transferring the knife to his clenched teeth, ramming the useless Henry into its saddle boot, sheathing the blade, refilling its vacated hand with a comforting fistful of case-hardened steel backstrap, worn grip screws, and well used walnut.

With the Colt out and ready for argument, a man felt better.

Even good enough for a twist in the saddle and an over-the-shoulder look at what he had behind him in the way of late afternoon callers.

Those boys were well mounted and making the most of the fact. They rode nearly as good as Kwahadis, which was to say the best in the Indian world, and had bigger, stronger horses under them than you generally saw with Kiowas or Comanches.

Well, if it was a horse race they wanted, they had picked a pretty good pony to beat. The black was a halfblood Spanish Arab from the best *caballaje* in Old Sonora. He was sixteen hands of horse and bred by a people who had been doing nothing else since they had dabbed a *riata* on the first of Cortez's wandering, Old World purebreds. He could go a distance at a quarter-mile clip or a furlong in fifteen seconds flat, and not be looking up the crupper of any Indian scrub anywhere in between.

And right about now those big Sioux ponies were giving him as tight a chance as a white man would ever appreciate, to prove it.

Ben rode the race the only way he saw it.

He let them get close enough up on him so that they could not cut across on him when he made his swing, then shot the black up the riverbank and headed him for the grove. Once up the bluff, he opened him out and let him run. Halfway to the grove he had his lead stretched to two hundred yards and was easing back in the saddle.

He didn't ease very far back. Once again he had sudden cause to remember the tenth Indian. That buzzard in the black furs had gotten down off his blufftop and back to his mount just in nice time to see Ben make his swing for the grove. And to spur his fast steeldust pony across the open flat to cut him off.

Ben cursed, flattened the black's belly to the snow. That red devil had him. All he could do was run for it and hope to Ka-dih he didn't get winged with a rifle slug on the way. His own Colt was useless at the range and the Sioux had at least one hundred yards to lever that Henry into him before he could get up to where the handgun would hold and hit.

He cursed again, wondering why in God's name those flat-hat fools in the grove didn't open up and give him cover. The wonder was father to the wish. No more had he cursed, than somebody from the camp began cutting down on the Sioux horseman with a repeating rifle. Even as the hidden rifleman fired, Ben had time for a last angry thought. What the hell were the rest of them doing in there? They had all had guns,

48

he had made sure of that before he left, even if he didn't recall the repeater that was letting off now being among those guns.

Anger as quickly gave way to admiration.

Whoever was handling that repeater had his eye flat down the barrel and knew how to hold on an incoming bird. He saw the snow fly close in under the racing feet of the Sioux pony on the first three shots, the mushrooming spurts beginning ten feet in front of the steeldust and walking dead into him. The fourth shot centered the pony, drilling him from brisket to breadbasket and dropping him, dead floundering, in his flying tracks. His rider rolled free, unhurt, leapt to his feet, ran doubled over for the shelter of his dying pony's belly.

Seconds later, the black was crashing Ben through the fringe trees, into the center of the emigrant camp. He was out of the saddle on the first slide, pumping fresh brass into the Henry as he ran toward the bunched wagons and the fur-clad figure of the lone rifleman beneath them.

The next instant he was diving between the wheels and dropping beside him, his whole attention riveted on the dead pony out toward the river. He snapped three shots, all he had had time to load, at the trapped Indian, making him dive back behind his fallen mount, abandoning any immediate plans he had for rejoining his henchmen in their retreat to the Arkansas redoubt.

"Cover the bastard!" he rasped to his companion. "I'm empty!"

"The *bastard*, brother," said the overcoated marksman quietly, "is covered. Load away."

Ben gasped. He twisted around on his propping elbow. He met and dropped his mouth open to the familiar, white-toothed flash of the cynical smile.

It was Nella Torneau.

Chapter Nine

WITH THE MAIN FORCE of the Sioux once more behind the banks of the Arkansas and pinned there by his and Nella's rifles, Ben had time to get his answer to the lack of fire from the emigrant camp. The place was a shambles. What his first-chance glance around it didn't tell him, the low voice of Nella Torneau did.

"They showed up about an hour ahead of you, mister," she said. "They rode straight in and stopped their ponies about fifty yards out. That brave in the black skins is their leader. He put his rifle under his leg and held up both hands, *real peaceful.*"

Ben chucked his head. This girl knew a thing or three about Indians. A man could tell it by the way she twisted her pretty lips around that "real peaceful," like it was powdered with alum or straight saleratus. He let her go on, wanting her to get shut of it, knowing she'd feel better when she had.

"He jabbered in Injun for a spell. It wasn't Caddo or Comanche. I couldn't make it out, and of course none of my folks knew a Kiowa from a Kwahadi."

Ben looked at her, wondering at her easy use of the southern tribe names. "Sioux," he said. "Northern Oglala."

She nodded, hurrying on. "Anyway, after a bit he gave up and said something to one of his little friends, big, darkfaced buck wearing a handful of black feathers. This one had been to school, a Reservation Injun for sure. He let us know in something that was aimed at being English, and missed it pretty wide, that they meant us no harm and only wanted to come in and get warm; and to maybe share a cut or two of our mulemeat.

"Not knowing them, and all, my folks wanted to let them come along in. Right about there, my friend," she straightened her mouth with the short nod, "is where yours truly headed for the wagons."

"It figgers," grunted Ben. "Go on."

"I dug Baby, here, out of my bedroll and took over the meeting." With the reference, she patted the beautifully engraved little Henry Repeater, giving Ben only time to wonder where she had gotten such a gun and what she was doing toting it in her personals, before concluding with a wry smile. "I reckon I raised hell and put a good-sized chunk under it. My

50

folks folded and the big buck with the black feathers did like-wise. At least he did after I'd thrown two shots under his pony's belly."

At this, Ben scowled. Damn the flat-hat fools. There was one thing they never learned. That was never to let any Indian outfit, made no difference how friendly they let on, come into your camp. Give them food, blankets, tobacco, anything you had—but never camp room.

"Where was you raised?" he said quietly to Nella Torneau.

"East Texas, mister. The Trinity River brakes."

He nodded, threw a shot toward the riverbank, narrowly missing a careless Oglala head. "You seen your share of red-guts, I allow."

"And more. My daddy had a little ranch outside Cold-spring down in San Jacinto County."

"Know it," Ben said "My pap drove cattle from down that way before the war. Your pap runnin' cows?"

"*He was.* He let a bunch of Caddo bucks into the house one day. I wasn't but three or four at the time—"

Again Ben nodded. In the old days Texas was full of Indian orphans. "I reckon I've heard the rest of it," he said. "What'd the Sioux do jest now, when you called 'em?"

"Threw in, like I said," she shrugged. "But holding a kicker like Injuns always do. They pulled around, went maybe ten yards toward the river, spun back and came for us." She gestured, indicating the fringe of the grove to their left. "I got two," she said.

Ben's eyes, following her direction, widened. Past the trees in the snow, already partly buried by the drifting wind, lay two paint ponies. From beneath the drift mounding one of them, a buffalo hide boot protruded stiffly. Ten feet from the other a third, smaller drift was growing. From it protruded not only a boot but two red hands and the distorted half of a darkskinned face.

"I'm one up on you," was all he said. "I got three."

"It leaves seven," said Nella.

"Agin two," agreed Ben.

"Three," corrected the girl. "Jed Bates is still alive."

"Whereabouts?"

"Upstairs." She poked the wagonbed above them with the Henry muzzle. "I got him bedded down in there after he was hit. He was still shooting up to a few minutes ago."

"Bad hit for sure?"

"For sure. Arrow. Still in him. Clean through both lungs, six inches out the far side."

"He's done then."

"And lucky," said Nella, hardfaced.

"How was it with the others?" asked Ben gently.

"Bliss and Johnson and Miz Bates got it easy, all down in the first rush. They got clean into us before I got my two and they pulled out. On the way they caught Tom Hudgkins with a lance. Miz Bliss and Tom's wife got crazy. Ran out to where they'd gotten Tom. That skinny devil with the red blanket cut back and got them both. Clubbed them down, first, then shot them on the ground. I was empty, he got off before I could bring down on him."

"That quick, eh girl?"

"No more than a minute, start to finish."

"Reckon I better have a look at Bates," said Ben. "Watch the river. And don't let that son back of that down pony so much as take a deep breath, you hear? We got him right where we're goin' to be needin' him."

"For what?" said Nella bitterly.

"I allow you'll see," muttered Ben, moving for the wagon's tailgate. "The bastards have took the first pot but they've played their red ace into a fair bad hole."

As the afternoon wore on, Ben's red ace began to look less comforting. He had figured the Indian wouldn't stand the intense cold of the pre-blizzard frost for more than a couple of hours. Would shortly be in the mood to make a deal for his freedom. But twilight was coming down and the Sioux hadn't peeped.

There had been a short, shouted conversation between him and his followers back of the riverbank, once the trapped brave saw the white riflemen meant to keep him pinned to his dead pony. After that the hours fled silently, with no sight or sound from any of the waiting Sioux. With dusk shrouding the grove and the snow at last beginning, Ben knew he had stretched his bluff for more than it was worth.

But weak or not, a man had to play his hand the way he held it. Ben played his by stepping suddenly out beyond the edge of the grove, calling to the braves behind the riverbank. As he did, he placed his rifle carefully on the ground before him, showing he meant to talk peace.

Shortly, the tall brave came up out of the riverbed, his black feathers slanting, flat out, on the drive of the bitter wind. He kept his gun in his hand but made no move to use it. In his guttural, thick-tongued English, he inquired of Ben what inspiration was stirring the white brother's imagination.

Ben told him. The white brother would allow the red-blanket brave to leave his dead pony and go free. In return he and the brave white squaw would expect the same courtesy, in addition to a twenty-minute start and the loan of one of the mules. The other four longears and the fine shelter of the white man's wagons would be generously left to the red brother.

The black feathered brave politely submitted that he was no fool. Let the white brother know that ten minutes after he arrived, their leader had opened the belly of his pony with his scalping knife and crawled into its warm paunch, had been since, and still was, quite comfortable. The snow was coming now, the darkness not far behind it. With such cover the red brother would take his chances of getting those mules and that fine, warm camp by his own devices. Was this all understandable to the white brother?

Ben admitted that it was, adding that when they came in to take the camp, they had better bring their best war charms with them. Some of them would be needing them for the long ride into the Land of the Shadows.

The big brave shouted back that now indeed everybody understood everybody. He was turning to drop back over the riverbank when the Sioux behind the dead pony called out to him. He stood listening to his leader's instructions for a moment, shouted once more to Ben.

Red blanket wanted to know the name of the white brother in the grove. He saluted him as a brave warrior, and thought he must have some red blood in him by the way he fought and talked. He would like to know what name to remember him by, what tribe to credit for his courage.

Ben thought a moment, knowing they had him where the neckhair grew short. And knowing that barring more luck than any two white people could hope to hold in the face of seven stormbound, starving Sioux, he and the girl had maybe twenty minutes between them and that yellow sign he'd seen on that buffalo skull. The thought to the contrary, the grin which suddenly twisted his wide mouth was as quick and crazy as any Clint had ever managed.

"*Sat-kan!*" he shouted back to the brave. In Kwahadi it meant just about the pungent value he presently placed on Ben Allison's future—horse dung. And was as good a name as any other, present company considered.

"And your people?" called the tall Sioux.

By now, Ben was feeling the wildness that was in him. The

53

dark streak he had always shared with Clint. That he had fought down all his life, and fought it so hard down that not even Clint knew he had it in him. That feeling that grew in a man's guts, low and cold and swift, when he knew he was backed into a one-way corner and had to kill his way out of it.

He stepped forward, over his rifle, the vacant, meaningless grin flashing darkly. Leaning down, he drew a ten-foot line in the snow, marking it with a broad series of wavering curves, like the track of a diamondback in deep dust. "The Snake That Travels Backwards!" he shouted to the watching Indian. *"The Tshaoh!"*

"The Tshaoh!" echoed the big brave, clearly impressed.

"The Enemy People!"

"That's right, you Throat Cutter bastard!" yelled Ben, still grinning. *"The Comanche!"*

Stepping back, he picked up his rifle, waved it airily at the brave. "What's your skinny friend in the Three Point blanket call hisse'f? Jest for the hell of it now," he added. "Seein's we're all gittin' so goddam cozy."

"Tashunka Witko!" shouted the brave defiantly. "Remember it when you die."

There would come a time when Ben would indeed remember that name. At the particular moment he was not quite ready to lie down and roll over, and he had never heard of Tashunka Witko.

"You've got a big mouth, brother!" With the return yell, he slipped back into the cottonwoods. "Let's see you fill it with somethin' worse than wind for a change!"

When he rejoined Nella, the wild grin was long gone, the pale eyes narrowed seriously.

"What the hell was *that* all about?" queried the gaunt-faced girl. "You can sure talk when you want to, mister. I never heard such a mess of nothing in my life. *Now* where are we?"

"They're funny," explained Ben quickly. "You give 'em a good fight, they think you're great. No matter they mean to take your hair for your trouble."

"Well," said Nella caustically, "you've played your little red ace and had it called, flat. What do we do next? Pray for a long sunset and two troops of Union Calvalry?"

"Pray for ten minues of good shootin' light," grunted Ben abruptly. "And throw some of that leftover mulemeat in my hoss's saddlebag."

54

"You can't mean to run for it, mister! We wouldn't get out of the trees."

"Mebbe I cain't," said Ben. "Nonetheless, I do. Jest the damn minute the snow's heavy enough to cover our backsides on the way out, you hear? That'll be likely about twenty seconds before they hit into us from all four sides. Git that meat into them saddlebags, goddam it. And rustle your blanket roll out'n the wagon and lace it on back of the saddle."

Nella started out from under the wagon, moving quickly now, in wordless, whitefaced obedience. Suddenly, she stopped.

"What about him?" she gestured toward the wagonbed above.

"He's all took care of," said Ben. "Git goin'."

Nella looked at him narrowly. "Wait up, mister," she demanded, face going hard again. "I thought you said we couldn't move him and that to pull the arrow out would kill him."

"That's right," Ben rasped.

"I'll not leave him!" cried Nella defiantly. "He goes, or I stay."

"He's a'ready gone, ma'am—" He softened it a little, seeing how it struck into her.

"Thank God," she breathed after a moment. Then, quietly. "Jed was a good man, he was good to me. And everybody. He just didn't know Injuns—"

"He sure didn't," said Ben.

"I'll get the meat and the blankets," Nella murmured. He saw the white teeth bite into the tremble of the full lip. "And thanks, mister, for seeing to Jed. I'm beholden to you that he went easy."

"Not quite, Miss Nella."

The soft, sharp way Ben said it brought her around, low voiced and staring.

"What do you mean—?"

Ben pumped two shots into the dead pony out beyond the grove, threw another three into the darkness now rolling toward them from the river bank. He levered the last empty out, already reloading as he rolled to his feet and faced the girl.

"Nobody," he said hoarsely, "goes easy agin a broadhead buffler arrer pulled out through his lungs, barbs backwards."

Chapter Ten

THERE WAS NO PURSUIT from the grove. The reason was white and cold and it was bucketing through the air about them at a nice, steady, forty-mile clip. It wasn't a full blizzard, just a medium rough spring snowstorm. The wind was due out of the north and a man could set a course by it and make fair slow time by holding to the high ground along the east-west ridges, staying south of their crests, naturally, to be out of the wind.

But the black gelding was packing close to three hundred pounds. By midnight, Ben felt him beginning to stagger and sensed, through his clamping knees, the flutter and tremble beginning to wrack the big ribs. At the same time the wind started to rise, the temperature to drop.

"The hoss ain't goin' to last it to the fort," he told the girl. "We got to hole up."

She tightened her arms around him in a way that put a thrill through him, cold or no cold. She pressed her head closer against his broad back, the quick tones of her voice letting him know the words were coming through that bright, hard smile.

"Mister, you're doing fine. Just find your hole, I'll crawl into it with you."

He turned the black up and over the ridge, heading him for the Arkansas. They were about halfway to the fort, roughly opposite the spot where he had seen the buffalo skull earlier in the day. Along the river at that point he remembered having seen a high clay bluff based with willows and honeycombed with wind and water holes. The base of that bluff would be shelter enough and he reckoned they might even find an undercut or a cave that would do even better.

He reckoned right.

Old Ka-dih was still with him.

The spot looked like just another watercut under the bank at the first sight of it through the storm-dark. But once down off the horse and feeling into it, a man could tell it ran on back under the bluff into a regular cave. Nor was that all. Last spring's high water had stacked up a dam of driftwood in its throat that would, if necessary, last them for firewood from now on until the ice went out.

He helped Nella off the black, careful and gentle about it

56

as if she were a child, and thinking as he did so, how many men could have stood up to what she'd seen in the past hours. And faced it through without a whimper, the way she had—with her eye lining up a Sioux buck down a rifle barrel half the time, and her arms hanging on back of a frozen saddle through fifteen miles of ice and wind the other half.

His own arm, circling her shoulder in the darkness, guiding her in under the bluff, tightened with the thought. She felt the pressure, instinctively sought for his big hand. Finding it she clung to it, the trusting touch of the slender fingers feeling to Ben like they'd wrapped themselves around his heart rather than his hand. They were back under the overhang now, out of the wind and the lash of the now. He stopped then, all at once confused and clumsy-feeling inside. "You set here along the wall," he said gruffly, pushing her down in the darkness and pulling his hand away from her. "I'll be back directly. Got to see to the hoss and fetch in some wood."

Outside, he fumbled an armload of wood out of the drift-pile, carried it back under the overhang, struck a light and got it going clear and strong. With the firelight pushing the blackness back and out into the willows, he led the gelding in under the bank. Pulling the saddle, he slipped the bit and bridle. While the big horse nuzzled his arm, he slid his hand along the crested neck, back and down across the steaming flank. Satisfied he was not too lathered to cool out safely without blanketing, he gave him a final pat and low word of assurance, moved off and let him stand.

The weary gelding didn't shift a hoof, only shook himself out, eyed the fire, blew the snow out of his nostrils, whickered gratefully, dropped his head and went to dozing in the reflected heat of the driftwood blaze.

With his horse taken care of, thought Ben, a man had best look to his woman. He grinned as the thought struck him. *His* woman? Now there was a hell of a note. What put a thing like that in a man's mind? It sure wasn't anything she'd done, or said. Or that he had. Well, no matter, he had to look to her.

Turning to do so, he saw what he should have known he would—Nella Torneau looking to herself.

While he was fussing with the horse, the girl had lugged in more wood, banked the fire, shaken the snow out of the bedroll, toted the saddle back into the cave, fetched out the mule-meat, produced a small sheath knife from under her wolf-skin coat, gone to slicing off pieces to roast over the flames.

Looking down on her, Ben grinned again. "You sure you

ain't part Injun?" he asked. "You work faster'n a Kwahadi squaw."

"When in Rome," said the girl soberfaced, not bothering to look up from her slicing, "ride with the Romans."

"Meanin' I'm a damn redskin," said Ben.

"Close enough to it," she nodded. "Cut me a couple of green sticks."

He went out into the willows, cutting the required roasting sticks and not thinking very much about what he was doing while he was at it. Right then a man didn't have mind for much except how funny it felt, and how deep-good, to be ordered around by that cussed big-eyed girl in there past the fire yonder. He ducked back into the cave, as schoolboy-grateful to be there as if he'd been gone a month.

"Miss me?" he said, and for no damn reason he could think of at the moment.

She looked up quickly, studying the shadow of quizzical soberness crinkling his eye corners.

"I knew you'd be back sometime this winter," she smiled. "Help me off with this coat and get out of my way."

He took off the coat, moved back out of her way and shouldered off his own. By now the place was toasting up warm and proper. While she spitted the meat and began to broil it over the flames, he dropped to his haunches, eased back against the warming clay of the wall with a contented sigh. Presently, he shifted his glance from the girl, surveyed, with a growing sense of restful satisfaction, the cozy interior of their Arkansas boudoir.

The cave was perhaps twenty feet wide and seven or eight high at its outer opening within which the black stood dozing. It narrowed to no more than six feet where he had built the fire and where the girl was now tending the mulemeat. Back of the fire it opened out again into a regular room, small, about ten-by-ten, and very low ceilinged, maybe no more than four or five feet. Its floor was of clean, dry river sand, the red clay of its walls showing no hint of seepage or dampness. The backflung heat of the fire fed snugly into it, while what little smoke there was worked its way along the higher slope of the outer opening to dissipate itself among the wind and the willows beyond.

Ben brought his eyes back to the girl by the fire. He nodded to the growing, drowsy warmth of the cavern and to the sizzling, crisp burning aroma of the mulemeat. About now a man could look up to old Ka-dih and mutter a word or two in what little he remembered of Kwahadi, by way of belated thanks.

58

Ben did so now. But the offering was not limited entirely by the brevity of his Comanche vocabulary.

He had never seen Nella Torneau out of the bulk and clumsy bundle of the trapper's coat. He was seeing her out of it now. The prospect put Ka-dih and the cave and the crisping mulemeat as far from a man's mind as the last star out.

She was dressed, not in emigrant homespun or frontier linsey-woolsey, nor yet in prairie fringe and buckskin, but in a soft checkered, settlement calico of cool green and pale tan. Under the dainty ankle length of the city frock's hem, the crude cowhide farmer's boots bulked large and ludicrous. But also appearing below that Sunday-go-to-meeting hem was something neither oversize nor out of place—the slim, trim, frothy frill of a lace petticoat.

But even the airy undergarment could not keep a man's eyes long off of what it was clinging to.

The girl, for all her gauntness and spring willow tallness, had a body under that calico print. And that body was anything but underweight.

The way she was kneeling to the fire, quartering away from him only enough to be unaware of his watching her, and the soft, clean calico tightening over her breasts and buttocks as she moved, while the shifting light of the fire caught and highlined every curving line of her, made a man think about something far removed from getting to Bent's Fort tomorrow.

She looked over at him, dark hair mussed and tumbled from the removal of the fox fur parka, face flushed, eyes squinted and frowning against the heat and smoke of the fire. If she had caught him staring at her, she gave no sign of it. She brushed back the loose forelock of curls, waved the smoking chunk of mulemeat toward him. "Come and get it, mister." She broke out the swift, sharp smile. "Before I throw it to the woodpeckers!" With the gesture and the smile, came the low laugh, the clean white teeth flashing behind it.

Suddenly, Ben laughed too. It sounded strange even to him. A man couldn't remember the last time he had done that. Laughed like that. But then, he couldn't remember the last time he'd been happy, either. "Don't throw it, ma'am," he grinned. "I'm on my way."

She looked at him as he came to her side and took the willow stick. "Mister," she said slowly, "you laughed. I never allowed you could."

"Miss Nella," he smiled, settling back against the wall and unsheathing the Kwahadi knife, "I done it and I'm glad."

She came to him, sitting crosslegged beside him, so close the tumbling hair brushed his shoulder.

"Mister," she repeated, holding his eyes through the little pause, her voice so low he barely heard it above the sudden hammer of his heart, *"so am I!"*

He banked the fire, building the sand of the cavern floor carefully around its base, covering its coals with heavy drift chunks and with snow brought from outside the entrance. The wetted wood simmered, settled into the glowing firebed. Watching it a moment, he nodded. It would dry out and burn down through the night, leaving a live heart of coals for morning and keeping the back cave toast-warm, meantime.

The thought of the back cave made him restless.

The girl was taking a long time. A man wanted to give her all the time she needed to get herself decently bedded down and covered up before he came in and rolled into his own blankets. He had figured she would want to undress with the cave so warm and dry and with her probably not having been out of her clothes for the best part of a week. But there was a limit to a man's patience once he was thawed out and full of roast mule and the godblessed peace and quiet of the place. And warmed through, too, in a way no fire could do it, with how she had looked at him and told him she was glad he had laughed.

He shook off the last thought, knowing from long experience how lonely people in a common tight, and shut off from all else, naturally drew to one another, meaning nothing by it that wouldn't dry up the minute they were back where others were around them.

No, the girl had meant nothing by the look and the words, nothing except that she was glad they were alive and safe and had each other to talk to. That was all, there wasn't any more. He'd go in there shortly, sleep the storm away, get up in the morning, take her on into Bent's Fort and never see her again. She'd forget him before he was out of sight down the south trail, would go on following her own hard-eyed way wherever she was letting it take her, and never think again of a lonely Texas boy named Ben Allison.

He tried to shake off that thought, too. Tried to make himself think he'd forget her just as quick, maybe quicker. He had a one-third piece of something bigger than anything most men even dreamed of. His next year's work and the bright trail of the years past that were laid out ahead of him. He had plenty to do, little enough time to do it in. He *had to* forget that girl and he would.

The high resolve held just long enough for her voice to melt it away. "All right, mister. I'm ready if you are. Bed's made and turned down."

He felt awkward now. Like he was about to walk into a strange girl's bedroom. And that she'd be afraid of him and what he was thinking and what he might try to do.

"Reckon I'll set outside here a spell," he muttered hoarsely. "Fire's goin' to need watchin' till she banks down and settles in. You go on to sleep, I'll be along shortly."

He thought he heard the low bubble of the laugh, but wasn't sure. "Come along now, boy. Don't be bashful," she called softly. "I'm all tucked in." She added the last like she knew he would want to be sure she was.

"All right," said Ben, feeling himself tremble all over with the word. "You got your coat in there? I'm goin' to throw mine over the hoss."

"I've got it," said the girl. "Come along in and tell me goodnight. I'm like to float right away for being that drowsy—"

He came away from the black and was ducking through the inner opening then, crouching over to fit his six feet four under the low curve of the ceiling. A moment later his eyes were adjusting to the reflected glow of the fire's shadows.

Beyond him, he saw the dim-lit warmth of the little room —and within it, the waiting, single bed of the wolfskin coat and her carefully tucked blankets. He felt the thick-lashed, sleep-lidded impact of her strange blue-violet eyes, sensed in them a primitive pleading that put the dark blood drumming in his ears. He heard, muffled and faint and wordless, the murmur of her husky voice.

She reached a slender arm, bare to the rounded shoulder, from beneath the blankets. She did not take her slanted eyes from his, as the reaching hand sought and found his corner of the bedding. The full lips fell apart and waited there, wide and warm and hungrily beckoning in the half darkness. Her eyes still holding his, the slim hand moved suddenly downward, bringing the blanket back and away from his side of the bed—and startlingly back and away from a part of hers.

Beneath the turned back cover, wickedly naked upon the deep, rich pile of the wolfskins beneath it, he saw the long, slow movement of the sinuous, rose-pink body.

"Tell me goodnight!" she whispered fiercely. Then, strangely soft, shadowed with loneliness, haunted with desperate longing—"

"And tell me that you love me!"

Chapter Eleven

BEN AWOKE SLOWLY, mind groping back from a long, happy way off.

When a man has just put under eight hours of the first solid sleep he's had in three days, his thoughts don't jump open quite as fast as his eyes. But the smell of roast meat and a driftwood fire are familiar prods to a plainsman's memory. He rolled up on one elbow, seeing the empty bed at his side, hearing at the same time the sounds of the girl moving around outside. By the time he got into his clothes and stumbled sleepily through the low entrance, things were coming back to him with a rush.

He was given no chance to put them into grateful words.

"Fetch out my coat, please." The nod was civil and no more than civil. "And bundle up the bedroll. Your meat's by the fire, yonder."

He looked at her a moment, wanting to say a hundred things, not able to think of any one of them.

He went back into the cave, got her coat, rolled the blankets. He was back out at once, determined now to have his say and get it off his mind.

Again, he had no chance.

Nella was throwing the forty-pound saddle on the black, making no more of the effort than would any knowing hand. "You eat, pardner," she ordered. "I'll lace on the blankets."

Ben sat down against the wall, confused, upset, wondering: beginning, too, to get a little riled. He ate the mulemeat, saying nothing, thinking much.

Well, if she didn't want to talk about it, a man could allow that figured, somehow. Maybe she was a mite upset for her own part. Maybe she was feeling the same as him, not knowing any better than he did how to put it to words. Let it be for now. It would come out soon enough.

It was a wise idea and a bad guess.

The miles marched along under the gelding's long stride. Nothing but smalltalk about the clearing weather and the remaining distance to the fort interrupted their swift passage. With the morning well gone and Bent's crowded post lying hard around the near bend of the Arkansas, Ben could stand it no longer.

"Nella," he grunted over his shoulder, "ain't we got suthin' better to talk about than what happened to the snowstorm?"

There was silence for the next fifty feet of trail. Then her voice came clearly enough. "Ben," she said deliberately, "just forget it."

It was the first time she had used his name. Hearing her say it aroused a whole new flood of thoughts in him, all of them rising around that wonderful hour in the cave. "That's a outsize order for a ranch boy," he said doubtfully. "Mebbe you kin answer it better than me."

"I can," said Nella.

Her voice wasn't hard now; still there was no hesitation in it.

"A woman's lonely and grateful and maybe a little scared and feeling bad-lost into the bargain. There's a fire and warmth and the first shelter and safety she's felt in might be a long time. Add a few kind words from a decent, clean-thinking man and you've got what happened last night."

"That all you got, Nella?" He said it quietly, trying to keep it level and easy. The girl didn't miss the rough catch of the hurt in it.

"It's all, Ben," she answered softly. "A woman like me's got only one way to pay a man she's beholden to."

"You wasn't beholden to me for nothin' at all. And you wasn't *payin' me* last night. Not no more than you was payin' yourse'f, you hear?"

"I hear, Ben, but I'm not listening anymore. Forget it like I said. There's no good in it for either of us. Believe me, boy, I've been there before."

"I ain't," frowned Ben. "I ain't never been there like that before. It don't make for easy forgettin', you hear me now?" He paused, reining the black in. He twisted in the saddle. "Nella," the name slipped out as easily by this time as though he'd been saying it all his life, "I want you to stick by me. I reckon I need you more'n any man ever needed anythin'. How about it, girl?"

He saw the shadow darken the violet eyes. Then saw it as swiftly disappear behind the dazzle of the bright, hard smile.

"Ben, are you proposing to me?"

"I reckon," he stammered, blushing hard. "Least-ways, the best I know how. Will you have me, Nella?"

The smile went the way of the shadow in the eyes, fading swiftly.

"I've had you, Ben," she said slowly.

"Meanin' you don't want no more of me."

"I didn't say that."

"Say what you mean, then. Straight talk walks the shortest distance."

She looked at him, shrugging helplessly. "All right, Ben, move the horse along. It's cold here in the wind."

He turned away from her, kneed the gelding, held him down to a chop step as Nella talked. They were only a short distance from the fort now. But it was only a short story she told him. Short, and not quite sweet.

When she finished, he let the silence grow for a long time. When his answer came at last, it was filled with all the child gentleness he had shown her the night before. Riding with his back to her, he could not see the return of the quick shadow to her eyes.

"I don't care where you been, Nella. Or what you been. Nor where you was goin', or aimin' to keep on bein' once you'd got there. A woman's got to live, same as a man. We ain't no different, you and me, in the ways we've went about it."

Quickly, then, he told her of his own past, softening nothing and concluding abruptly. "We both picked the easy way and found it harder than the hubs of hell. It ain't no sign we got to keep runnin' on dry axles. A month ago, up in Montana, I took a new trail. Mebbe it'll lead me summers, mebbe it won't. But it's a chance, girl, the best I've been give. I'm askin' you to take it with me. To leave me split it with you, fifty-fifty. And nobody askin' no questions about nothin', from here on out. What you say?"

"I say keep the horse moving," said Nella Torneau huskily. "You were headed south when we met, me, north."

"Don't riddle me none," pleaded Ben earnestly. "I want a straight answer."

"You've got it, boy." The quickness and the sharpness were back in the low voice. "I'm still heading north."

The week at the fort passed. On the good, handcut winter hay and eastern rolled oats, there available, the gaunted horses rounded out quickly. With the morning of the eighth day they were ready to travel.

Throughout the preceding days, Nella had not weakened to Ben's increasingly hesitant persuasions. She insisted she would stay at the fort, continue her original way north with the first arriving of the spring emigrant outfits. She refused to wait for him until he returned with the herd, or to travel on with him and Clint and Stark to Fort Worth. He made his last, fumbling plea the night before the start, came away downcast and carrying a weight of heartsink and loneliness that kept him tossing till daybreak. He had seen Nathan Stark approach the girl shortly after he left her, thought nothing of it except to tell himself, of a sudden, that he didn't want any man around her but himself. That was a small idea and he knew it. He had it pretty well fought down by first light, too. But the thought of leaving Nella was still hard and heavy inside him when the sun rolled up the long valley of the Arkansas.

Within ten minutes after it did, he knew he was *not* going to leave her. Not then, and not ever.

He walked away from the black, leaving him half saddled and whickering curiously, went straight to the post sutler's store where she had been staying. He was in time to see her and Stark come out of her quarters, laughing and talking.

Fighting down the black anger that rode up in him, knowing it wasn't really black, but green, he waited until Stark left to see to his own preparations for departure. He stood awkwardly before her, not answering either her cheery good morning or the familiar, too bright smile that came with it.

"Nella," he blurted out, "I ain't leavin' you."

"Bad news sure travels fast!" She surprised him with her quick sarcasm. "How'd you know?"

He started to answer, suddenly realized what she had said. He had meant to tell her he was leaving Stark and Clint, giving up his share in the herd. Would go and gladly go, with her, wherever the trail might lead, north or south.

Instead, he stepped back, eying her uncertainly.

"I don't get you, Nella," he muttered.

"That's right, Ben, you don't." The smile brightened unbearably. "Mr. Stark does."

Ben's jaw set, bad and hard.

"Now don't get up on your back feet and start waving your paws around like a damn bear," she laughed. "I'm only agreeing with you, boy. Like you said, you're not leaving *me*. I'm goin' with *you*."

"I'm right glad, Nella." He said it simply. He wanted to shout for joy, but Stark was sticking in his mind, stopping him. "What's Stark to do with it?" he tailed off bluntly.

"He talked me into it," shrugged Nella carelessly. "Offered me a job I can get by on, that's all."

"What kind of job?"

"Not the kind you're thinking," she said easily. "A good job."

"Sech as?"

"Dealing faro. Some saloon up to Virginia City. Black Nugget or something like that. It won't be the first girl that's tried it, you know. Stark reckons the boys'll give my table a big play," her tone turned defensive, "and besides, he paid me in advance!"

She faced his growing scowl, concluding defiantly. "I can *deal* cards, too, mister! Open a snap. Pass a buck. Sweat the deck. High, low, jack and game. Ten, king, deuce, or trey. You name the game, I'll deal it."

It was one too many for Ben. At the moment his stumbling mind couldn't get far past the main, happy fact that she was going with them. And mostly it didn't want to get *too far* past it. To the waiting girl he spoke just what was in his heart, not shadowing it with any of the clouds beginning to build up behind his thoughts.

"Nella," he said softly, "in my game you could never deal anythin' but double aces—"

The trusting worship which, as Ben had so clumsily tried to tell her existed in him for Nella Torneau, grew only deeper and more dear with each long mile southward.

The girl was a never ending wonder to have along, never losing her cynical good nature, never tiring on the trail, always quick to see her share of the campwork and to pitch into it without complaining. After a few halfhearted male attempts to dissuade her on the shaky grounds of cow country chivalry, they gladly enough let her alone, and mighty grateful when all was said and done to shut up and enjoy a woman's cooking for a change. Most especially such a woman's!

Never did delighted frontier "dancehall girl" endure so much sincere attention, nor get swarmed under by such an eager surplus of flour-sacked centaurs and bow-legged, high-booted fire tenders. None of them could help her enough, and the competition at dishwashing time was little short of disgraceful. Even the aloof Nathan Stark unbent after the first few camps. Long before they crossed Red River the staid Virginia Citian could manage a batch of baking powder biscuits or a boiling of red Texas beans with the best of them.

Clint, of course, was in his element, playing the dashing knight errant of the plains to the handsome hilt. If he was not rampant on his sorrel mare performing his endless repertoire of south plains horsemanship to the applause of Nella's breathless glance, he was mooning, couchant, on the starlit turf of the fireside spinning her gargantuan Texas lies of his singlehanded victories over entire Union Army corps, or his never ending, Sir Galahad-pure search for the soft-eyed, virtuous southern belle who would one lucky day be Mrs. Clinton Allison. He mixed his extravagant metaphors and perverted the seamy facts of personal history with such an entire and skillful skipping of the busty blondes and broken bourbon bottles which in truth composed his main claim to fame, that even the taciturn Ben was half wondering if he really knew his sometime small brother. Further, Clint had not had a drink since leaving Virginia City. A man could happily see, Ben allowed, that like himself the kid felt so good to be back in the *illano estacado* he just naturally wore himself out being his rightful, sweet-natured self. Then, too, you couldn't miss the fact that the nearer they got to home, and as they began passing the outlying ranches with their open range, deep worn cattle trails and their distant, faint-bawling bunches of grazing steers, the more Clint began to take stock in and ask questions about the doubtful scheme he had so grudgingly allowed himself to be declared partner in.

It was a short, happy time for all four odd-mated travelers. Good feeling and optimism were over the bank and into the willows by the time they forded the Big Wichita River and swung east to bear down on Fort Worth. In fact, the five-hundred-mile stretch from the Arkansas had so dried Clint out that in the last camp out of Fort Worth, on the West Fork of the Trinity, Ben actually caught his brother joking with Nathan Stark—and being joked right back at.

Ben had said no more to the girl, nor been given the chance to. But she had played it so cussed straight the whole of the rough, ten-day ride that a man had to forget his being shrugged-off and discount his worry about what had been said and done between her and Stark. And, forgetting it, just set back and wonder that there was such a girl anywhere in the whole wide West. And to think to himself with no little honest pride that no place but Texas could have bred her kind.

The last day's sun came booming up out of Louisiana and across the North Sabine River like it couldn't wait to get them on their way. Ben welcomed its five o'clock prying under the face cover of his black hat by rolling out of his blankets and yelling-up the rest of them like he was heading a two-day schoolboy hike over to Blue Mountain or Weatherford.

They were long gone down the last miles, south, before the sun got high enough to pull a man's shadow halfway under his horse. Ahead of Ben Allison, as far as the sun-burned squint of his pale eyes could reach, lay nothing but wide open, easy prairie and a bluebird, east Texas, April morning. That, and the sweet red dust and spring sweat of the coming herd gathering.

Clint, totting the too slow fall of the southern miles between him and the Big Town, couldn't see far enough ahead, and not fast enough. Nor get any picture out of the brillant April sky save the glistening mirage of the big sourmash bottle beckoning him over the last rise, yonder.

Nella Torneau, squinting to the same sun and south-reaching miles, saw only as far ahead as the easy swing of Ben Allison's broad back, only as far behind as the blank set of Nathan Stark's blunt-jawed face.

The man from Montana, peering expressionlessly southward, saw past and farther than any of them. Beyond Ben Allison. Beyond Fort Worth. Beyond the coming herd. And, seeing what lay there, nodded silently to himself.

All things come to him who rides last.

Nathan Stark was an old, old hand at handling the drag. The point and swing were for more reckless men, and simpler ones. Let them have it. Ride last, always last. Say much, mean little, do nothing. And wait.

Chapter Twelve

THE FOUR O'CLOCK DAYLIGHT, running up gray and still from beyond the Sabine, made black skeletons of the maguey and cholla cactus. Its distant thinness brought the fading, farewell yelp of the last coyote retiring with the dawn.

The two horsemen sat their mounts on the low barranca overlooking the Big Bend flatlands of the North Trinity. Below them, as far into the river bottom mists as the peering eye could carry, restless with the spreading movement and musical bawling of the morning rise, the vast herd was getting to its feet.

Above the ground-deep rumble of the longhorn horde's lurching, rump-first rise, the jingling tinkle of the bellmare echoed briefly: the night wrangler bringing in the daymounts. Across the stirring herd, the mushroom string of the chuck and bedding wagons cleared and grew distinct against the silhouetting blackness of the river willows. Shortly, the cook's breakfast fires were pushing back what little of the darkness remained in the Trinity's sprawling bend.

Clint fought down the awesome ferment of a stomach which, like Lazarus, would not lie down and stay dead. He strained his tortured eyes once more across the packed ranks of the great herd, saw, unhappily, that the cattle were now beginning to mill and push out demandingly against the thin circle of cursing riders who sought to hold them hard bunched in the bend, and to prevent them from breaking out and beginning to graze.

The wayward half of the Allison frères had spent the last night, none too figuratively, in Fort Worth's ample bosom. He had ridden into the holding camp three blind staggers and a bourbon stumble ahead of the dreaded coming of the sun. He was, accordingly, in no mood and less condition to face a weanling calf, let alone three thousand tailed up, travel-ready mosshorns.

His cotton-mouthed inquiry of the nobler brother expressed the doubt succinctly, if somewhat sourly.

"Well, 'Sam,' now you've gathered your three thousand precious goddam San Saba steers, you got any deathless bright ideas what in Christ's everlastin' name you want did with the bastards?"

"Just one," said Ben Allison tensely, excited mind and sweeping gaze far from Brother Clint and the evil belly of the morning after. He straightened in the saddle, standing ramrod thin and tall in the stirrups. His glance swept for the last time across the angry bellowed, horn tossed dust of the bedding ground. Then, deep voiced, he flung the long delayed excitement of the order to the waiting cowboys below, his narrow face flushed and dark with a fierceness Clint had never seen there.

"Let 'em go!" he shouted wildly to the watching cowboys. Then, black hat swept off in wide-arched, armflung finality. *"Point 'em north—!"*

That spring of 1866 was wet. Chickasaw Billings, at fifty the oldest man in the crew by twenty years, could remember nothing like it. Every stream was either up or on the booming rise, and the leaden, mud-slogged miles between rivers were literally "waded" by the exhausted cattle. Clint, staying on his pony to grab his supper off the chuckwagon tailgate, rather than get down into the hub-deep slop washing past its wheels in the rain-driven darkness, chose a half-floating camp three days north of the Canadian River to open an impromptu forum of unprintable Texas opinion.

"This here, gents," he called across the slash and winnow of the rain between him and his bedraggled companions, "is the first friggin' herd ever to swim from the San Saba to Sedalia without techin' bottom."

"Shut up, and don't git the salt wet!" snapped Saleratus McGivern, grabbing the battered shaker from Clint and sheltering it to his flour-sacked bosom.

"I allow," continued Clint, unabashed by the dough wrangler's assault, "that we ain't seen their feet fer six weeks. But I kin tell you, gents, they ain't clove no more. They're webbed like a goddam mallard's, and I seen three big dun steers yestidday was sproutin' fins along their dorsal verteebrays and whippin' their behinds from one side t'other like a bigmouth bass goin' upstream in shallow water."

"It's the gospel," solemnly averred Charley Stringer, a wizened hand from Uvalde County. "I went to strip a fresh heifer was bawlin' to be milked this mawnin' and so he'p me I got four and one-half gallons of grade-a cavvyair."

" 'Tain't nothin' to what I seen on night herd long about two A.M. yestidday mawnin'," drawled Waco Fentriss. "You all know how blamed stubborn a damn steer is, how the bastards'll lay down on you wherever you stop 'em, no matter
70

what's under 'em? Well, after a couple of circles I seen the main herd was purty well bedded down, there bein' no more'n two foot of water runnin' acrost the high ground they was held on. But yonder out in the middle of the main bunch I seen a wide patch of water, open and clear it was, and a b'ilin' and a bubblin' away somethin' fierce. Well, I pushed through to where it was and sure enough no sooner did I git there than my damn hoss stepped off the edge of an arroyo, puttin' us clean under in ten foot of water."

Waco paused, blankly eying the bounce of the rain in his empty plate.

Slim Blanchard, bone-wet, weary, suffering alike from the incessant rain and six weeks of grease-fried food, belched the expected query more in relief to acid indigestion than interested curiosity. "Well, what the goddam hell is so remarkable about that?"

"Nothin', nothin' atall," shrugged Waco pleasantly. "But I must allow it's the fust time I ever see three hundred head of cows bedded down clean under water like that—and every last one of them sound asleep with a long stem of hollowjoint grass stuck in their mouths a'breathin' out it atop the water. You see, it was them there breathin'-straws of their's was settin' all thet bi'lin' and bubblin' I seen out in thet open water."

"If there's anythin' I cain't stand," lamented Hogjaw Bivins, "its a goddam, lamebutt Lampasas liar. No more imagination nor real understandin' of the wonders of nature than a son-of-a-bitchin' toad. Them three hundred steers *you* seen," he sneered at Waco, "wasn't usin' them hollowjoint grass stems to breathe through. They was employin' them to put oxyjen into the cussed water so's them four hundred head I was holdin' directly under your three hundred wouldn't have to come up for air. Fact is, old hoss, them steers of yourn was standin' on the shoulders of mine."

"Well, anyhow," broke in mild-eyed Luke Easterday, a thirty-year "oldster" from Paint Rock, "I reckon neither of you got clean to the bottom of that draw or you'd have saw me and my eight hundred as was—"

"Likely," Clint interrupted in righteous indignation to Luke's claim, "you're about to say you was the son of a bitch had them eight hundred standin' on my twelve hundred. Now afore you fly up and puff out, jest remember we ain't got but two hundred head left and the water's gittin' deeper all the time."

"I reckon," philosophized the defeated Waco, "that you are right, and that likewise the fust liar don't stand a spavined chance. Besides, you're Ben's brother and couldn't tell a lie. I do allow, howsomever, we kin all agree she's been a tolerably moist spring."

So ran the trail, the good Texas tempers rising above the bad weather, the tough Texas owners of those mercurial spirits taking all that a northern God who was certainly no patron of once-Confederate traildrivers could throw at them.

There is little ground to be gained lingering over the trail-side evils which befell the first five hundred miles of Ben Allison's adventure. The thunderstorms raged one atop the other, each new earth-shaking rumble and sky-forking lightning bolt starting a fresh stampede. What little of the way to Kansas the cattle didn't swim, they ran. The grass, coarse and stemmy from the torrential downpours, would not make beef and the herd was soon rib thin and runny boweled from its reedy keep.

The only known trail up and across the panhandle plains was the one they presently followed, the Sedalia Trail, leading to Missouri and the Mississippi River markets.

It was Nathan Stark's plan, soberly opposed by Ben, to follow this trail to the Kansas line before turning west and north. The Montanan argued that if they were to find themselves with a herd that could not be pushed farther, they could at least sell out to the Missouri buyers and avoid complete ruin. It was a hard business view, not to be argued down by a simple Texas cowboy's hunch that the herd would have been better drifted straight across the unknown Indian Territory. Nonetheless, Stark, carefully fair about it, put the matter to a company vote. The drive crew, conscious of the raunchy, failing condition of both feed and herd, their eyes on their paychecks and the hell with making history, voted Ben down.

Now, nearing the Kansas line, the great herd slowed. Then, within two days, stopped altogether.

Ahead of them and on both sides, east and west, as far as dust-reddened eye could see, stretched an endless, milling jam of longhorns. The grass, for as many miles as Ben and Stark could ride in the late afternoon of that second day, was eaten to its dying roots, and the incessant, hoarse bawl of hungry cattle was as strident and miles distant at midnight as it was at high noon. Before dusk fell that second evening, Ben counted no less than twelve big herds damming the trail ahead.

After a wordless, hurried supper, he and Stark rode out to

the nearest camp. Their blunt questions brought equally abbreviated answers.

The outfit they were talking to, and all of those in the trail beyond, were Texans. Clearly, Stark & Company had not been the only boys west of the Big Muddy with the idea of cashing in on the northern, greenback-belly for good beef. Every ex-Confederate cowman in the Lone Star state that was hale enough to straddle a cutting horse and could raise credit enough to put a herd on the road was currently holding his mortgaged cattle between them and the Kansas line. There were no less than two hundred and fifty thousand head packed in ahead of them, and some boys, who had ridden north to the last camp, guessed it at half again that many. Call it a quarter of a million, mister. You'd be on the safe side by sixteen herds and nobody calling you a liar.

And why, you say? Why all the jam-up? What had happened to the Sedalia trailhead? Simple, mister. Ever hear of the Jayhawkers?

Ben nodded darkly.

What Southerner hadn't?

If Quantrill, Todd and Bloody Bill Anderson with their Missouri Irregulars had earned the gratitude of the South through their guerrilla operations along the Kansas border during the late war, and had earned in the process the dread title of Missouri Bushwhackers, certain sanguinary gentlemen from the free state of Kansas had rated equal bloody distinction serving the cause of the Union—and been dubbed for their efforts Jayhawkers.

Jennison, Jenkins and John Brown were names as dark with hatred of the South as were Quantrill and the others bright with Dixie's misguided, guerrilla love.

The rest was grimly succinct.

The border war, *sub rosa* and savage, was still on. The remnants of the southern guerrillas headed by the lately risen triumvirate of three unknown newcomers, Jesse and Frank James, and one Thomas Coleman Younger, were being hunted down throughout Missouri's Clay and Jackson Counties. The Jayhawkers, outlawed alike with their Bushwhacker counterparts by the surrenders of Nashville and Appomattox, had sought eagerly and with quasi-official blessing, for southern fields upon which to vent their recently acquired trades of murder and extortion.

They had fallen upon a hell-sent, defenseless answer in the flood of Texas cattlemen rolling up the old Sedalia Trail.

There were probably a dozen jayhawking crews in operation along the line, numbering in the many hundreds of desperate membership. But the prime bunch was that headed by the sinister Alvah Jenkins.

Their game and its rules were simple enough.

For Texans, and any number could play, those rules were precisely, three. Rule One: a man could stay with his herd doing nothing, and watch it starve on the eaten-out range south of the blockade. Rule Two: he could pay a passage tax of two dollars a head and move his cattle on through to market. The third rule, which the hotheaded southern cowboys had instantly drawn up when faced with the first two, was the simplest of all. A man could, if unsettled enough between the ears, oil up his belt guns and drive on through, blue-belly bandits be damned and three cheers for the Stars and Bars.

Of the first six outfits which had played it according to Confederate Hoyle, one had outdealt the stacked Yankee deck and made it through to Sedalia. Five others were last seen starting north, had evaporated, along with all their cattle, somewhere between Montgomery County and the Big Muddy. The odds were questionable, even for Texans.

Rule One being out, since no cattleman could sit by and see his stuff die for want of grass where there was aplenty of it thirty miles north, and Rule Three having been killed aborning, Rule Two, the pay-and-pass-on option, had been briefly tried. A dozen outfits had scraped up the bribe, gotten through to the Missouri and Iowa buyers above the line, found that their stock, watery-grass thin and grading three cents better than wolfbait, would not pay out the added two dollars a head.

The owners, madder and wiser and in hock over their sixteen-inch Texas boottops, had drifted back through the congested camps on their ways south. The word they cursed and left behind for what it was worth, was get out and go home and leave the goddam cattle where they stood. There were up to three hundred thousand steers log jammed against the Jayhawk deadline, and at two dollars a head they weren't worth driving to the next creek let alone to St. Louie or Des Moines.

It was a darkfaced Ben Allison who sided Nathan Stark on the silent ride back to the wagons.

They were not only cut off and trapped in the backhouse. But if they didn't move fast, and damn fast, they were apt to find the stinking shanty shoved over on top of them, with them left standing up to their ambitious ears in what was under it.

Chapter Thirteen

NOT COUNTING STARK, there were twenty-odd men in his drive crew; eighteen fulltime cowboys, two horse wranglers, a cook and two halfbreed assistants, a jack-of-all-trades farrier and graduate of doubtful *cum laude* "cow doctor," and Ben and Clint Allison. Not barring Nella and excepting only Stark himself, every member of the Montanan's trail outfit was as deep-Texas as range beef and refried red beans.

And, again excepting Stark and the girl, the sum total knowledge of that Texas delegation could be spelled out in three capital letters; thusly, C-O-W, with the "c" silent, and pronounced "beef."

Herd bulls, heifers, sack-wet calves, weaners, long yearlings, four-year-old market steers, six-year stags and ageless mossyhorns alike, they were all "cows" to the Texas hands. If they knew another word they never used it and when they said cows they meant "beef."

Beef, and the cows that made it, composed their entire lives and learnings.

It followed that when Ben called them up around the late coffee fire on his and Stark's return to announce that the herd faced disaster, they were set back on their dung-caked heels. Hard looks went asking at ten cents a dozen and the sudden shiftings of sagging cartridge belts and old vintage Navy Colts could have been offered at a nickel a gross with the market flooded in the first twenty seconds of their trailboss's report.

To a bowlegged man they were ready to fight. Ben Allison, previous higher education on getting himself and his, out of corners limited to the six-shot course taught in the old University of West Texas, was more than ready. Should the distinguished class of '66 feel impelled to go ahead with its present evident intent to buck Rule Three and bet into the Jayhawkers' pat hand, he would gladly open the pot by riding point for the gamblers from Fort Worth.

But once more, quick and brainy as ever, Nathan Stark graded-up to the class Ben had always figured him to have.

The big Montanan stood up, waiting for the men to quiet down following Ben's fight talk. When they had, he looked at the latter and said very quietly, "Ben, you or Clint, or the first, next man to follow you, will have to walk over me."

On the trail, Stark dressed in workboots and plain buckskins, wore two .38-caliber Navy Colts, crossbelted. Ben had no more idea than the last man across the fire whether or not the blondbearded young giant could use those Colts—had, at the same time, certain satisfaction that he *would* use them.

"Well, we're waitin', Mr. Stark," he suggested softly.

It was the first time Ben had "mistered" him in weeks. Stark took note of it, kept his words to the point and his back to the chuckwagon.

"You're not making sense now, Ben," he began patiently. "You know I won't listen to you when you don't. Boys—" He turned soberly to the silent crew. "I've got ten thousand dollars of my own money tied up in this herd." It had been part of the original agreement that Stark would be announced owner of the herd, and Ben said nothing. "Now Ben, here, sounds like he meant to shove it all in on a gamble to beat the Jayhawkers, and I figure Clint will back him."

"You're a whiz at figgers," grunted Clint, lounging carelessly away from the wood wagon.

Ben at once slid forward.

He had seen his brother's mouth loosen and that far-away, quiet look of half humor and no-humor-at-all start to get into his eyes. The time to watch Clint was when he started to look like he wouldn't pull fuzz off a peach. That time was right now.

"Clint," he warned. "Hold up and listen to Mr. Stark. Comes to cows, it's you and me. Comes to money, it's him. You hear me, now?"

Clint eyed first him, then Stark. "Ears widespread as handles on a slopjar." He nodded laconically to the latter. "Pick me up and pee me full."

"All right—" Stark passed it off like there wasn't any dry grass around and he hadn't seen the sparks about to fly. "I simply propose we ante-up to those outlaws. It will let us get the herd through and sold. That way we can guarantee wages, and with me the men come first. You do it your way you'll take such losses you won't be able to halfway pay out."

Clint lost his grin. Stark wasn't talking to Ben, no matter he was looking at him while the words came out of his mouth. He was talking to the men.

The Virginia Citian now paused dramatically to prove it. He wheeled from Ben, faced the waiting cowboys. "Boys," he said humbly, "I don't care about my share except to see that you get yours. I know Ben means you the same and doesn't aim to sound like he's trying to do you out of anything.

Clint shot a side glance at Ben. "Brother!" he hissed under his breath, "I'm about to kill myse'f one mealy-mouthed Montana bastard."

"Hold tight, you hear me, boy" rasped Ben. "He's only makin' sense the way he sees it. Same as he allus does. You jest don't listen."

"You mean you jest don't *hear!*" snapped Clint. "You big dumb slob, Ben. Cain't you see he's makin' a goddam hoss's butt out'n you."

"He's makin' sense. The only way he sees it," repeated Ben stubbornly. "Leave him be."

Clint subsided mutteringly, moved back against the wood wagon.

When he did, Stark concluded modestly. "We'll take a vote," was all he said.

The men talked earnestly among themselves for fifteen minutes. Meanwhile a rider loped out to the cattle to collect the opinions of the boys on nightherd. On his return, Chickashaw Billings, quondam elder statesman and self-appointed Mother Superior of the drive crew, stepped uncomfortably forward.

"She's thirteen-to-five," he drawled sourly. "Me, Waco, Slim, Hogjaw and Charley Stringer sees it like Ben. The *others,*" there was no escaping the persimmon sneer with which Mr. Billings rendered the social distinction, "sides with Stark. I allow there ain't no end," he glared at the unhappy traitors, "to what some sons uh bitches will do fer money."

Sensing the makings of a first-class fight without going one step out of his own camp to find it, Nathan Stark poured on his best pint of peace oil.

He turned to Ben, gesturing in frank appeal.

"Ben, what do you say? Are you willing to go along with the other boys and me? I want you to, you must know that. You've brought the herd this far when none of the rest of us could have done it. I'd like to see you take it on through. But you call it the way you see it. And either way, Ben," he finished quietly, "I reckon I don't have to tell you how you stand with us."

Ben tried to think. On Stark's side lay cold logic and common sense, on his own, only angry instinct. Stark was likely right and him, dead wrong. On the other hand, what about the Gallatin Valley and that million dollars in three years? And all that big talk the night they'd thrown in with the Montanan's big dream. Something was wrong about Stark's talk just now. Something a slow man couldn't get his hand on, but could *feel* all the same. Something in what he said, or in the way he said it—

Frowning, Ben looked up to find Nella Torneau staring at him across the fire. The girl had come up unnoticed by the main group, to stand with Clint in the shadows of the wood wagon. Confused as well as angry, Ben's first bitter thought was that she'd drifted up to wait out the argument so as to be sure to pick the winner. She'd been a lot with Stark lately, had not had much time for him. It was like her hard kind to just stand there and watch them both without a blink. And wait to see which one she would wind up smiling at.

But the eyes of the Trinity River girl never wavered, and suddenly Ben knew she was not looking at Stark, or Clint, or anybody else. She was looking at him, Ben Allison.

Timpas Creek came back. The cave on the Arkansas returned. The long, happy ride to Fort Worth. The talk on the ride to Bent's Fort. The hundred hard, bright smiles. The precious scant few of long, soft ones. The low-voiced words and the soft, wide lips that had uttered them there in that Arkansas darkness. All these things came back now, swift and sudden and bell clear. And with them returned the slow, certain order of Ben Allison's mind.

He and Stark had both been wrong.

A man read that now in the flash and challenge of Nella Torneau's violet eyes. And read it just in time. Go on! those eyes were saying. Don't quit on me now, Ben. You said you would never leave me. Follow me now, Ben. Follow me always. *North, Ben, north!* Remember—?

"I reckon," he said at last to Stark, "you and me has both been thinkin' a little short. I was jest reminded of suthin'."

"Go on, man," said Stark uneasily.

"Montana," said Ben. And he said it and meant it for Nella Torneau.

Stark knew it. He had not missed the exchange of heated looks between the girl and his towering trailboss. Typically, his face remained expressionless, his blue eyes, steady.

"We're a long way from Montana, Ben. You should have thought of that at Red River crossing."

"I did," said Ben. "And was voted down."

The blue eyes darkened. "You were," said Stark. "And were again, not five minutes ago."

"Comes a time," Ben's drawl turned warningly soft, "when votin' won't do it."

Stark stepped past the warning in flat-voiced stride. "I take you to mean that time has come——"

He broke off the statement to step slowly back and away from the fire.

In the ordinary course of such impasses in the Southwest, the next words would have been spoken by Colonel Colt. The present course was lifted out of the mundane realm of six-gun averages before either Ben or Stark could make his opening hammer-thumbed remarks.

Standing as he was, outside the firelight and facing north, Ben saw them first. And seeing them, he eased the forward hunch of his right shoulder, let his tensing right hand fall slack. He only grinned suddenly at Nathan Stark. His two-word answer came with the wave of his left hand toward the darkness north of the fire.

"It has," he said simply.

They all saw them now, and heard, suddenly, through the following big stillness, the creak and jingle of their saddles as their crowding mounts halted five yards beyond the fire.

As Ben had said, there came a time when voting wouldn't do it. That time had not come the way he was thinking of at all. But it had come. And in a way that left none of the late cowboy constituency in doubt of the parliamentary outcome of any debate likely to be held in the next sixty seconds.

Thirteen-to-five, or any other way you wanted to recount it, as of right now Stark & Company were outvoted. And the next election bid well to be balloted Ben Allison's way—with bullets.

There were no less than three dozen heavily armed guerrilla horsemen standing their sweated ponies short-north of the chuckwagon fire.

Not too long ago there were grizzled oldsters still mending saddles or swamping out bunkhouses in northern Montana who could tell you, from having been there, of the following three minutes around that Kansas campfire. The main idea you would get from their rheumy-eyed remembering would be that Tom Horn and Bat Masterson and Butch Cassidy "wasn't in it" with a certain tall, quiet boy from San Saba Texas.

Stark opened the pot by stiffly demanding names and a stating of business from the guerrilla visitors.

He got both, back-to-back.

Three of the bearded ruffians shoved their horses farther into the firelight. Their leader, a stocky, pasty-faced youth of twenty, hooked his jackbooted leg around his saddlehorn, shifted his quid of longleaf Burley, spat into the fire, delivered himself to the required information.

"You're lookin' at Carter Jennison, yours truly," he bowed mockingly. "And Simm Webb and Burris Walker."

"Any relation to 'Redleg' Jennison?" inquired Ben civilly. He was referring to the hated war leader of the Kansas Union guerrillas.

"We're kin," scowled the youth, not liking the plain inference in the big Texan's wry-mouthed query. "Where's that leave us?"

"Waitin' to hear what's brung you down on us poor defenseless southern boys," interrupted Clint smilingly. He moved up with the answer, siding Ben but standing well away from him.

"You won't need to wait all night," sneered the youthful Jayhawker. "We're from Alvah Jenkins, you may have heard the name. Jenkins sends you his love and suggests one of you ride back with us, with somethin' in yer saddlebags besides hardtack and jerky. The goin' price is two dollars a head, suckin' calves admitted at half price. We're told you're drivin' close to three thousand head but Alvah's an easy man and likes round numbers."

"All right, Jennison."

Stark stepped toward him.

"How round?"

"Five thousand dollars, gold or greenbacks."

"We haven't got it. You'll have to take a draft."

"So? That's interestin'. What bank?"

"The Mastin Bank, Kansas City."

"Could be. Sounds all right. It's fer Alvah to say. . . . You comin' now?"

Stark opened his mouth, but it was Ben Allison the words came from.

He said it soft and he said it slow. And after that the softness and slowness had had their play for the evening.

"No, you Yankee bastards, *you're goin'*."

The sneer was still on young Jennison's mouth when the .44 slug made it immortal. Simm Webb was fast. He got his righthand gun almost clear of its leather. And only almost. Clint's three shots bucked into him, all in the belly close under the heart, nearly tearing him in two. The third guerrilla, with the advantage of the split second Ben took on Jennison, got one shot off. It was wide of Ben by a foot, and for a very solid reason. In the instant of its discharge, Ben's second and third shots were shattering his cheek and collar-bones, respectively.

The blast of the Texas brothers' .44's was still slamming back and forth between the close-parked canvas walls of the chuck and wood wagons when its uproar was cut through by the backing volley of five interested fellow Texans.

Old Chickasaw Billings was first into action by a shade, but Waco and Slim would never admit it. For their tardy parts, Charley Stringer and Hogjaw Bivins later apologized to Ben, with the latter insisting his first two snaps hung fire and the former declaring that Chickasaw bumped him in the stampede for shooting room.

In any event and in somewhat less than three seconds after Ben's first shot spread Jennison's sneer by the precise dimension of forty-four one hundredths of an inch, eight good Texas hands were filled, and the fire going across the camp-site into the packed ranks of the stunned guerrillas was assaying about thirty ounces of lead to the foot.

There was a scattered, wild sprinkle of shots from the outlaw band, but with their horses pitching and jamming into each other and with their three leaders dead and down in as many blinks, they never got into effective action.

Ben hastened their inclination to depart by kicking the campfire into a shower of flying cottonwood embers, plunging the battleground into the questionable shooting light furnished by a bad combination of starlight and stringy wood-smoke. Abetting his quick-booted decision, and using the time it gave them to change their votes, the negative thirteen who had stuck by Stark now sought to make up for their treason to the Lone Star cause by working overtime and without wages.

Their combined talents were several too many for the scattering guerrillas. Stark & Company were shortly left to tot up their casualties—three bulletholes in the chuckwagon, two in the canvas of the wood rig, one through the treasured, indignant felt of Chickasaw's twenty-year-old beaver hat—and to assemble forthwith for another quorum on the question before the house.

In the swift melee, Nathan Stark had seized Nella, shoved her behind the wood wagon, gotten back out only in time to stumble across a saddle in the darkness created by Ben's kicking the fire out, and fall heavily against the iron-bound hub of the wagon's rear wheel.

He was still rubbing the side of his head and not talking when the new vote went against him, twenty-six to nothing, with Nella Torneau, slant, violet eyes all for Ben Allison, abstaining.

In the darkness, the men ran swiftly for their saddled night horses. The wagon teams were run in, backed and cursed hurriedly into the trace chains. Not a man argued Ben's chilly prediction that daylight would bring Alvah Jenkins and his two hundred Kansas Jayhawkers down onto them and their cattle. The idea right now was to put as many miles between their half starved herd and the Old Sedalia Trail as could be brought off before first light.

There was one direction those miles could be made in, and only one. Ben Allison had called it for them, as short and hard as he had called Carter Jennison.

West—and due west.

Straight as a Texas crowbait pony could fly, fast and far as a scared San Saba steer could run.

Chapter Fourteen

THE GUERRILLAS did not follow. The notorious Jenkins may have had several reasons, any or all of them adding up to business acumen: his profession was head-taxing Texas cattle, not getting his tangible assets killed off by unreconstructed Southerners.

As far east as Ben could see the following, sunbright morning, not a dust cloud disturbed the fair Kansas skies.

And the good luck held.

Once safely away, Stark resumed unquestioned command of his herd. He held it for five days, at which time he proposed a continuing direct route for Denver, then north along the Rockies, up and across Wyoming. Once more, Ben bowed his sunburned neck. This time Stark reasoned and flattered to no avail. His tall trailboss would not budge. And for reasons he had picked up en route from the guerrilla clash.

The scattered settlers they encountered driving west along the state line were unanimous in the warning: the northern Sioux were out, raiding as far south as the Smoky Hill stage road, and had succeeded in persuading their southern cousins, the Arkansas Valley Cheyennes, to join them in their unholy war. Cause of the outbreak was a chain of new forts the army was building north of Fort Laramie, straight across the Sioux Treaty Lands.

Though Ben had a Texan's normal unhealthy contempt for the average Indian, he had had a slight taste of these northern redbirds at Timpas Creek. He felt he could comfortably do without a second helping.

Countering Stark's suggestion, he insisted they drive, roundabout, back to Fort Leavenworth, Kansas, start all over again from there. While it meant taking the cattle six hundred miles to gain two hundred north, he got Stark to agree. They were on wonderful grass now, and the herd was picking up tallow fast. The time lost in going back to Leavenworth would be gained back in hard pounds of good beef made on the way. Leavenworth was the main army post west of the Missouri. Stark had freighted from there five years, knew every officer above second lieutenant in the state of Kansas. They could get help and outfitting there that would not be possible on the Denver route. They could move the herd as far as Laramie under army protection, getting at least that far without worrying about the Sioux.

These were tall arguments. Stark had no glib answers for them.

Two hundred miles west along the Kansas line, past the last settlement marked on the Montanan's army maps, they swung the herd north. Another two hundred miles and they turned the cattle east again, retracing the original two hundred miles to arrive at Leavenworth six weeks after leaving the Sedalia Trail. There had not been a stampede. nor a single high stream to swim. The cattle were putting on weight, getting beautifully broken to the trail. The morale of the entire crew was high, the friction between Clint and Stark had worn away to a minimum.

But irreplaceable time had been lost.

They had been on the trail one hundred and forty days since leaving Virginia City. It was late May and fifteen hundred long, hot miles still faced them up the scorched valley of the Platte, along the old Oregon Trail and across the divide into Idaho Territory, then back over the mountains again to Montana and the Gallatin Valley.

Stark sensed the need for pushing ahead as certainly as did Ben.

In two weeks at Leavenworth, he worked the crew around the clock, buying and breaking new teams for the wagons, acquiring additional supply wagons and loading them to their topbraces, culling the herd for the long pull ahead, mending every piece of worn gear, shoeing each last head of workstock in both the saddle and draft strings.

Ben listened and watched and thought. And on the last day went to see Nathan Stark.

He found him supervising the loading of the last wagon. This was the "camp rig," a spanking new, lightweight Conestoga which would carry all the "personals" of the herd owners, and travel first in the long wagonline.

Swinging off the black, he nodded to Nella, who was watching the loading from the back of the beautiful paint pony Stark had bought for her from a wandering band of Pawnees. He thought the smile she flashed him was a little quick, but he had other things on his mind. He gestured to Stark, motioning him away from the wagon. When the big man came over, he put it to him.

"Leave a fair-size hole in that load, and leave me have a draft for a thousand dollars."

Stark laughed. He owed this long, tall cowboy plenty. But

didn't mean to pay him off quite like that. "Ben," he smiled, putting his hand to the broad shoulder, "I sometimes suspect that behind that cigar-store Indian scowl of yours, you've got the best sense of humor of any of us."

"Could be. Right now I ain't exercisin' it."

Stark sobered. "All right, what's on your mind?"

"Life insurance. Got a hankerin' to buy some."

"You're not serious, man!"

"Somewhat. Gimme the draft."

"Who to?"

"Robinson and Petty."

"The hardware firm at the post?"

"Know any other Robinson and Petty?"

"What are you buying, Ben? What is it you want?"

"Rifles."

"Oh, good Lord, man, we've got more than we'll ever need, now."

"Not like these, you ain't. Not you nor anybody else. There's none been seen like these out west. Neither by whites, *nor* Injuns."

At the slight emphasis, Stark's eyes narrowed.

"Go ahead, Ben. Make sense and the money's yours, you know that."

"We ain't talkin' about what *I* know. It's what *you don't*."

Stark shrugged. "As you've taught me to say in the words of your heathen Comanche ancestors," he smiled quickly, "*my ears are uncovered.*"

Briefly, Ben told him about the new guns.

They were breech loading, single shot Remingtons, built to a new patent developed by Philo Remington himself. The breech was opened by a rotating block system, called the "rolling block," which brought the block back and down to make reloading far faster than even the latest Civil War Spencers. And they used a new brass, integral cartridge, which was a vast improvement on the Spencer load. Enough of these trim new pieces in hands that knew how to hold on a galloping north plain's paint, ought to be just the medicine for dosing ambitious hostiles along the way.

"They cost twenty-eight dollars each," concluded Ben. "Robinson and Petty has got thirty of 'em, and I want all thirty. That and two thousand rounds of that new brass ammunition. It tots to jest one thousand dollars, even."

Stark looked at him. He had not known Ben had even been to the post since their arrival. Much less taken time to cover it thoroughly enough to dig up the new Remington rifles and all the information about them which he clearly possessed. This thin, pale-eyed Texas boy, with all his slow, soft talk and dumb, easy way of going about things, was something disturbingly more than the simple cowboy he let on to be. A man would have to refigure him, and watch him. And he should have done so, and been doing so, long before now.

To Ben, he only smiled again, stepped to the tailgate of the camprig, made out a blank draft to Robinson and Petty. When he gave it to Ben, he was no longer smiling, and his blue eyes were in their old, expressionless set.

"You know, Ben," was all he said, "you're not quite the man I thought you were . . ."

They did not follow the Oregon Trail as a matter of so many wagon ruts. Ben knew better than that. He had never been out the Old Road but a man had a fair idea what emigrant draft stock could do to a piece of grass from the time him and Clint had worked along the Denver route. And that was a pretty new trail. Given the twenty years since '48 and '49 that the goldrushers and landgrubbers had been using the Platte Valley to head out for Sutter's Mill or Whitman's Meadows, you didn't have to guess much. There wouldn't be a blade of decent graze nor a stick of matchwood kindling left within ten miles of the river, north or south.

He held the herd on a rough course between twenty and thirty miles south of the stream, found good grass and wood and water the whole way. Laramie was reached without incident. One or two bands of apparent hostiles were seen, far off and not hanging around long, and that was all. Nothing but hard work marred the drive, nothing but drudgery distinguished it.

Another eight hundred miles and ninety days were gone, that was about all you could say, with the latter figure being the only fault in the fair sky of their luck so far.

The day they struck the Laramie River, swinging the lead steers north along its east bank for the last eight miles up to the fort, was the 17th of September. When they bedded the herd three miles past the fort, at sunset, a man could know just one thing for certain: October, with its warning frosts bearding the sunrise grass and its six o'clock scum ice rimming the water barrels, was staring them in the face; and they were still seven hundred miles from Montana.

Yet a halt and rest were imperative. The trail cattle and workstock, alike, would need at least two weeks of open graze and clean Platte water to fit them for the last high drive over South Pass and the distantly frowning Rockies of western Wyoming.

That night, Ben rode with Nathan Stark to the fort, the latter to renew old acquaintances among the military staff, the former to mix with the post bullwhackers and enlisted scouts —and keep both ears open.

The question both herd owner and trailboss proposed to put was a hard one, dictated by the fact they were driving thirty days late, with summer gone and fall wearing frostily away: what were the chances of short-cutting the herd up the Bozeman Road, square across the Sioux's Powder River Treaty Lands? This, of course, was the route originally envisioned by Stark, but abandoned by him on advice of officer friends at Leavenworth in favor of the longer, safer route of South Pass and the Oregon Trail.

When, nearing midnight, he and his taciturn trailboss rode back toward the herd camp, they had both heard different expressions of the same bad news.

For Stark's part of the report, they had the unofficial good wishes of the U.S. Army, as indeed he had guaranteed the Texas brothers the night above Alder Gulch. But beyond the *sub rosa* extension of the wish, he got only a field-grade frown and the professional opinion that his chances of getting through were highly questionable.

Ben, receiving it from a less formal source, had been given a more colorful diagnosis of the same disease.

"You got," was the synthesis of opinion from the government teamsters and cavalry scouts, "about as much chanct of takin' three thousand steers and thirty men past the Powder as a mule has of brayin' without raisin' his tail." In delivering this, his version, to the scowling Stark on the ride back to the herd, Ben tailed off with an eloquently shrugged, "I seen many a mule bray in my time, mister."

Stark nodded, only adding glumly. "So have I, Ben."

For once, unequivocally, there was unanimity of Texas and Montana opinion. North or south, panhandle, Gallatin Valley, or waypoints in between, the much cursed, hybrid jackass son of Old Missouri always exercised his brasslined lungs with his shavingbrush tail aimed in one bullheaded direction —skyhigh.

"Well, Ben," said Stark quietly, "what do you say? Colonel Lamine, in command here, tells me Lieutenant Colonel Carrington is in charge up on the Powder. I know Carrington well. But Lamine says the Bozeman is shut down, airtight, north of the Powder. He said he himself won't stop me from using the Bozeman as far as Fort Reno, but that beyond that, Carrington's command takes over."

He paused and Ben said, "So——?"

"Lamine showed me Carrington's orders, right from old General Hancock and the Department of the Missouri Headquarters: positively no civilian traffic across the treaty lands. Ben, I said I knew Carrington——"

"Well?"

"There'll be no traffic."

"Thet ringtailed, eh?"

"A martinet, Ben. Garrison officer. Knows nothing about Indians or fighting Indians. Lives by the good book and for him that's not the Bible. It's *Field Service Regulations, Operations. Serial FM 305-58.*"

"You're real sure about that serial number, now?" grinned Ben.

"And the colonel that goes with it," replied Stark, not smiling. "Ben, I think we're licked. Maybe for good, north or south, but for the Bozeman, out-and-out."

"Uh-huh, could be. Where's this Carrington at right now? How fur north?"

"He's building a fort just beyond the Powder. Fort Kearney, I think Lamine said. It's about seventy miles north of Fort Reno, which is right around one hundred and seventy from Laramie. Call it two hundred and forty, all told."

"Interestin'," was the total of Ben's noncimmittal grunt. Then, thoughtfully. "This fort at Kearney about done, you reckon?"

"About. But he's got Fort C. F. Smith and two more to build yet north of Kearney, to garrison the Bozeman, Lamine tells me, right through to Virginia City. But until they're all done, nobody but army uses the road."

"Uh-huh. Well, I reckon we cain't wait on him and his forts, likely."

"Nor on the weather," said Stark uneasily. "Ben, we're getting into October."

The big Texan ignored him. "Now, accordin' to them army maps of yourn, the Bozeman is near three hundred mile shorter than South Pass, and considerable lower. That right?"

"Between two hundred and three hundred miles, yes. Lower by up to four thousand feet in places."

"And you still aim to take the long way round? And the high? Over South Pass, inter Idaho Territory and back acrost?"

"What else *can* we do, man!"

Ben looked at him, put it into one simple word.

"Fight," he said quietly.

Stark missed the softness of the way he said it. His thoughts were his own, and were turning on a phrase that had no place in Nathan Stark's history—financial failure. It was as though to lose money were an unclean, indecent thing. As Clint had sourly observed, after watching him haggle for the cattle with the Fort Worth ranchers: "He ain't got no more morals than a stray dog. I reckon he'd ruther see his sister raped than spend a dollar as wasn't guaranteed to git him back ten."

Thinking now of the herd beyond the next rise, Stark indeed was seeing dollar signs. At $35 a head on the hoof in Virginia City, he had a potential $100,000 bedded down a mile west. It was not in his lexicon of success to gamble that kind of money against the combined commands of Colonel Carrington's Regular U.S. Infantry and Red Cloud's Irregular Oglala Cavalry. He had, further, no intention of letting the gaunt Texan get back in charge of things this close to the final pay-off.

"Ben, be reasonable, man!" He tried for the old, now-just-leave-everything-to-me reassurance, and didn't quite make it. "We can't fight the army and the Indians, both!"

"Speak for yourse'f," said Ben stubbornly.

Seeing the way it was, Stark dropped all pretense. And dropped his voice, flat and hard now, along with it.

"I just have. We'll go South Pass."

"We'll go," said Ben, just as rock-flat and deliberately, "the opposite way we went at Red River and the Kansas line."

Stark stopped his horse. Ben pulled the black in. Neither man spoke.

Below them, in the five-mile swale of the Laramie's bending juncture with the Platte, the wink of the nightfire picked out the chuckwagon and the moving silhouettes of the first-guard shift of riders, just in from the herd and savoring the asphalt mix of Saleratus's midnight brew of Mocha.

"And how is that?" asked Stark at last.

"My way," said Ben Allison.

At the sunup breakfast fire the following morning, Stark found out which way was Ben Allison's.

With the herd on belly-deep grass and near clean mountain water, along with no wind or weather to move them away from either one, but four men were needed to ride circle. Accordingly, twenty-two Texas cowboys lounged around the morning fire waiting for Ben to speak.

He made it the best way he knew how—short.

"Boys, this'll be the last election. We got two ways to go south, over the mountains; north, up the Bozeman Road. The army says the Bozeman's closed and full of Injuns. Stark says south and the mountains. That way there's no army and no Injuns."

"Uh-huh," grunted old Chickasaw Billings, eying him speculatively, "and what *is* there, thataway?"

"Three hundred mile and thirty days out'n the way."

"So?" drawled Waco Fentriss, knowing it wasn't days and trail-miles putting the shadow in the tall boy's pale eyes.

"So, *snow*," said Ben shortly. "We git caught in South Pass crossin' over, or in Wind River Pass crossin' back, we lose our cattle a way I wasn't brung up to believe on."

"Which is?" offered Hogjaw Bivins.

"Without a fight."

There was a little pause then, after Ben had said it, not so much for thought as for speculation, Texas-style.

"I am constitooshinly opposed to snow," observed Chickasaw thoughtfully.

"I dearly love the boys in Union blue," admitted Hogjaw grudgingly.

"I'm deathly feared o' Injuns," fretted Charley Stringer. "They git you outnumbered better'n seven hundred to one, you ain't hardly got no more'n a fifty-fifty chanct of beatin' 'em. Less'n, nacherally, you got both hands free and a good-sized pile o' rocks handy."

"I hate a fight," shuddered the wizened Waco in righteous conclusion. "And wouldn't hardly never ride no more'n six hundred mile of bad trail to git inter a good un."

The little silence returned long enough for the venerable Mr. Billings to readjust his cud of Burley and park its accrued earnings in the middle of the fire.

"I allow, Benjamin," he nodded soberly to the elder Allison, "thet allus barrin' knowin' when we're gonna git paid, the next best flea thet's bitin' us is whereaway you got yore shifty leetle eyes peeled this fine mornin'?"

"Straight," grinned Ben, coming up off his heels with the laconic answer, and thumbing its due north direction over his left shoulder, "up the son-of-uh-bitchin' Bozeman."

Chapter Fifteen

BY STARK'S ARMY MAPS it was 169 miles to Fort Reno.

The way Ben rode it, on point with Clint the whole fifteen days of it, it was four government freight wagon burn-outs and the charred ashes of three big emigrant outfits.

The blackened wagonboxes and heat-twisted wheelrims of the latter parties were long weeks past their firing, the half-burned oak planks already mercifully sinking into the shadow of the summer grass, the wheel irons, bed braces and scattered tracechains red-scaled with fresh rust. But the last of the government freight parties was something else again.

Bodies keep well in the high, dry air of central Wyoming.

And these had not been too long in the keeping.

Where they buried the last of them, shallowly scooped into the thin soil, dignified only by a brooding cairn of loose rock, the tenuous, blue-white wisps of hardwood smoke were still curling skyward from the embers of the gutted Conestogas.

Ben rode quickly on with the burial party.

The herd dust was growing faint ahead, there was nothing more a man could do for the poor devils.

But in their staring eyed, twisting limbed stillness there was something they could do for him. They could tell him, without him thinking too hard about the yellow sign on that Arkansas buffalo skull, which of the red brothers had passed this way.

The variety and imagination displayed in the mutilations were pretty standard for the breed: some scalped, some partly scalped, some not scalped at all; an ear missing here, a forearm or foot, there; one, a pincushion of arrows in the bowels, another, a sieve of buffalo-lance holes through the kidneys, a third, leg-spraddled, with the genitals excised.

But all, and every one, no matter his other disfigurements, was bound to his dead fellows by one common brutality: the throat, opened and gaping from ear to ear.

The scouts at Laramie had told Ben much about the Sioux. Enough and to spare, for him to correctly read the stark sign around the freight wagon burn-out.

The northern Indians were not, unlike their southern Kiowa and Comanche cousins and in defiance of popular eastern belief, commonly given to mutilation of their victims. The burning pole, the rawhide rack, the sun stakeout, the ant heap and the hundred-and-one refinements of the art of doing in the white brother were not ordinarily for the taller, more patrician warrior of the north plains. When he did so stoop to conquer, a man could know that the last milepost had just been passed and that business as usual was out the Oglala window. Any step he took beyond the point of finding Sioux mutilations, he took with the certain knowledge that all the red chips were in the middle of the trade-blanket and that the next raise would likely be his own scalp.

About now a man could take some comfort in the fact that Fort Reno would be reached with tomorrow's drive. And while taking that comfort he could compound it with the uneasy thought that wagon burn-outs or otherwise, they had not seen so much as a Sioux feathertip or fleeting glimpse of distant paint-splashed pony, the whole of the one hundred and fifty miles behind them.

It was anything but a salubrious air which settled in over the little camp with the thin, quick chill of the Wyoming night, five hours later.

Stark and Ben sat long over the chuckwagon fire, watching and listening into the outer darkness. The former consoled himself with the repeated statement that the nearness of Fort Reno guaranteed their safety for the moment. The latter, not arguing the hopeful point, kept his thoughts to himself. Shortly after nine o'clock they had visitors. And shortly after that, considerable of the starch went out of the Montanan's self-stiffening optimism.

They both heard the cheery hail at the same time. Looking up, they saw an old man and a boy sitting their stout mountain ponies just beyond the fire's farther reach.

"Where in the devil did you come from!" Stark's indignant question exploded with nerves, and with the upset of the fact that two horses could be walked right into his camp past the pickets Ben had insisted on putting out every night since Laramie.

"Git down and come in, dad," invited Ben soberly. "Coffee's on and boilin' away." Then, curiously. "C'mon now, how'd you git past our boys, old salt?"

The old man was still smiling as he and the youth got down and left their reins trailing.

"Not much to playin' whites when you practice on reds," he shrugged. "Me and the boy, here, been a long time north of the Powder."

He was a trapper from the old days, before there was an Oregon Trail or John Bozeman had been born. The boy was

92

his grandson, raised by him when the Crows had cornered his parents up in the Three Forks country, "along about '59."

When he and the boy had eaten, the old man packed his short stone pipe, answered a few equally short, hard questions.

"Wal, now, it's thisaway," he squinted in reply to Ben's query as to what had put him and the boy to nightriding. "Ye see, I bin in these hyar parts a tolerable spell. Long enuf to know plumb nigh ever Injun south of Canady by his fust name. Ye treat 'em white and ye don't go to hoggin' on their buffler and ye stays a decent piece out'n their way, ye gits on with 'em and ye gits to know 'em. En they're funny onct they ever take to ye."

"Uh-huh," grunted Ben. "How's thet? How funny I mean, old-timer?"

"Wal, hyar's a case in p'int, me and the young un, yonder. Long 'bout three days gone, one of 'em rides up to our cabin one night. He gits down, hogs four, five pounds of our fresh buffler hump, he'ps hisse'f to three, four pipefuls of my longleaf, gits back on his potbellied scrub and grunts, *'Kola tahunsa he mani-mani.'* Thet thar's Sioux palaver fer, 'Friends, Romans and feller country-folk, take yerse'ves a walk.'"

Ben nodded. "Thet there *'mani-mani'* means *pasear,* thet it?"

"Wal, I lay it does. *Mani* means walk. When they double it up on you, they don't mean trot."

"The buck was tellin' you to git out, eh?"

"And fur out," grunted the trapper. "Likewise, some fast."

He paused, not grinning anymore. "Me and the boy didn't wait fer sunrise. We been a hundred and fifty miles since then. Got another hundred and fifty yet to Laramie, I calculate."

"On the nose," said Ben. "You see any Injuns on yer way down?"

"Country's thicker with 'em than screw worms in a heelfly hole. Never see it so bad since the Crows ris up and cleaned out Jackson's Hole."

Nathan Stark, silent through the brief exchange, now said quickly. "You and the boy better stay with us, old fellow. You'll be safer here."

"Youngster," said the old man eying him. "We're beholden to ye fer the supper, but I allow ye've got a sight to l'arn about redskins. The further'st place I hanker to be shet of is this hyar camp o' yourn."

He broke off the words to nod to the boy, and move with

him toward their drowsing ponies. Mounted up, he kneed his horse close in to the fire, accenting the observation with stabs of his stone pipe. "Anytime ye got more'n two white cow chips stacked in the same pile they'll draw Sioux flies till hell won't cut the crust they'll lay on ye."

"Hold up, old hoss," said Ben. "What Sioux we got in front of us? Oglala, ain't they?"

"Wal, now thar's some Hunkpapa mixed in with 'em but they're mainly Dirt Throwers, like as not."

"Dirt Throwers?"

Ben wasn't set on making a life study of the Sioux, but all a man could learn of them wouldn't be a shade too much for right now.

"Oglala," grunted the old man.

"I thought they was the Throat Cutters," said Ben, puzzled.

"Now, thet's the name fer any Sioux. Thet's what their Nation calls itse'f—Throat Cutters. They's six er seven tribes of 'em, all told. Thar's the Brûlé, them's the Burnt Thighs, the Hunkpapa, as calls themse'ves the Border People, the Wahpetons, Fallin' Leafs, and such like. The Oglalas is the Dirt Throwers."

"Obliged," nodded Ben soberly. Then, quickly adding. "Red Cloud's their big chief, thet right?"

"Old Makhpiya? Hell no. He's a *tame* Injun, mister. Been to Washin'ton, shook the Grandfather's hand, rid the iron hoss and all thet. Folks back yonder gen'rilly think he's the bad un, but he ain't by a fur piece. Out hyar, we know a heap different."

"How different, Old-timer?"

Somehow Ben knew his questions were getting close. He could feel, without being able to say why, that the last answer was going to be the big one.

"Young un," said the old man, peering long and thoughtfully at him. "You look to have a fair-sharp eye in yer haid." He turned his horse with the final nod, his warning coming back to them from the closing darkness beyond the fire.

"See you keep it peeled fer a raunchy leetle buck don't look no more like a chief nor a half-starved Osage squaw. Mean-skinny leetle bastard, allus rigs hisse'f out in a black wolfskin and bright red Three Point."

Ben's eyes widened, his mind flashing to Timpas Creek and back in the second it took him to come up off his heels.

"What's he call hisse'f?"

He shouted it quickly over the fire, into the darkness, the excitement in it narrowing Nathan Stark's eyes as suddenly as it had the tall Texan's. When Ben Allison jumped up like that, it had to be something.

Stark knew his trailboss.

The old trapper's answer, soft called and fading back over the clip-clop of his mount's departing hoofbeats, was indeed something. With a fair amount to spare.

"Tashunka Witko," came the muffled reply. And then, still farther off, just before all sound died away—*"Crazy Hoss!"*

Minutes later, with the late moon three quarters past full and smoky orange with the pocking shadows of old age, climbing wearily up out of the distant Big Horns, Ben came to Nella's tent.

It was a commodious, new, army shelterhalf provided by the solicitous junior officers at Leavenworth, and pitched now, as always, in the campside lee of Stark's lead wagon. Ben stepped softly as he came up to it, thinking to find the girl asleep and not wanting to awaken her if she was.

"Get down and come in, tall man." The soft voice startled him. He had not seen her sitting in the inky triangle of the tent's entrance. "We haven't seen you since the Sedalia Trail."

"Seems like it," sighed Ben, sinking to the folded buffalo robe beside her. "Herdin' cows is a forty-eight-hour job, I reckon."

"You've been wonderful at it, Ben."

He thrilled to the continuing caress of her voice. And thrilled, too, to the signal it gave him that he had come up to her in one of those moments of strange, rare softness she could show.

"Mebbe," he said awkwardly. "Mebbe not. Leastways it's all I got to offer. Somehow, it don't seem like much, lately. Not near enough, anyhow. I dunno, it's what I come to see you about."

"What, Ben?"

"You and me."

"What about you and me?"

He looked into the darkness, trying to find the words. "It's what I dunno, Nella. Mebbe you kin tell me. Where are we, girl?" he finished haltingly. "And where we goin'?"

"In Wyoming, boy." He could not see the smile, but he felt it. "Going to Montana, I hear."

"It's not what I mean."

"I know, Ben, I know—"

He didn't say anything, and presently she went on.

"You're good, Ben. Tall and strong and gentle and kind. And sweet, too, Ben. Inside-sweet, the way that gets into a girl, and deep into her, to where she can't see you without her breath pulls long and slow and her arms hurt and for no damn reason at all she wants on a sudden to let down and cry her heart out."

"Nella—!"

"Wait, Ben. I got to say it."

"Say it, then." He drew back, the sharpness in her voice warning him and holding him away. "Say it soft if you kin, Nella."

"Oh, Ben, that's just it. I can't say it soft. It isn't in me that way. I don't feel it like that. Ben, it's no different now than it was when you stumbled in out of the snow on that cussed black horse of yours. Nor than it was when you slid in under that emigrant wagon and yelled at me to keep the bastard covered. Nor than when you toted me in out of the wind and putting me down, and patting me and holding my hand the whole while like I was a little kid or something. Nor than when you looked at me like a wet hounddog somebody had kicked out of the kitchen, when I told you I was going to deal a table for Stark in the Black Nugget."

"All right, Nella—"

She swept on, not hearing his patient, tired acceptance of the way it was.

"No, Ben, nor than it was when you stood back out of the way all of that long ride to Fort Worth. Letting that crazy Clint make over me like a lovesick Comanche. And watching Stark ogle me and give me all that tall talk about Virginia City and what a hell of a swath he was going to cut through Montana, and letting on like half of it could be mine if I was smart enough to tell a big man from a dumb cowboy, and all such like. And you all the time looking at me like a rib-gaunted herd bull with the bellyache, not having sense enough to know where it was hurting you nor what to do about it. Nor yet being bright enough to get out of the way and go along when you'd been tailed-up and told off—"

She paused, breathless from the building emotion of the long outbreak. She took his hand in the darkness, suddenly, fiercely.

"Oh. Ben, I've tried not to hurt you. Tried to keep you from selling yourself notions I didn't want to pay off when it came my turn. I can't keep it up any longer. You're all that's good and sweet to me in the whole world, Ben. Oh, God! It isn't fair this had to happen to you—"

Ben looked away, and far away. To the Arkansas and back, slow-traveling every hurtful, heart-tug mile of it in his lonely memory.

"Nella," he said at last, "I came here to tell you I love you."

He had never put it in the words before. He felt her hand tighten suddenly in his, when he did. But the miles had grown too long for sympathy, the night too late for any hand squeezing. "I'm sorry." He went on, fighting down the sink and sickness inside him, keeping his voice down.

"Ahead, we got bad trail. It may be we don't make it through. I wanted you to know how it was with me, and will allus and forever stay. A man don't like to square into what we got waitin' fer us, uptrail, with suthin' like thet inside him. I'll allus love you, Nella. There ain't been none afore you. There cain't be none after."

He stood up then, but she did not free his hand. Instead, she arose with him, stood watching him, waiting and wordless. He hesitated a moment, helpless in that last dead silence after a man has offered his heart, only to have it handed back, and before he can bear to take it again and turn away.

"Thanks," he said at last, "for listenin' and lettin' me know."

There was no cynicism, no reproach in the way he said it. It was just goodbye in the best, honest way he knew to say it. "Git some sleep now, Nella, and don't fret about the Injuns, you hear? We beat 'em once, you and me. I reckon we kin do it agin. And jest fergit the rest of it, girl, you hear now?"

The moon was angling above the wagonsheets, then, slanting its waning light across his lean face. She saw the shadow of the remembered grin, felt its slow-turning edge twist in her heart.

"I reckon, Nella," said Ben Allison softly, "you don't have to shove the backhouse over atop me to run me out'n it."

He saw her smile, then. The old, quick, bright smile. And saw behind it in the same unbelievable moment, the moon-glitter of the black-lashed tears.

"Oh, Ben! Ben! You've still got it just as backwards and blind-wrong as ever. The moon's in my eyes, boy, look at me, Ben, look at me! Do I have to tell you—"

"Mebbe you do, Nella," he muttered hoarsely, hearing and seeing her, not able to believe it, or not daring to. "You said you didn't want to hurt me no more. I—"

Her hands slid to his shoulders, the soft weave of her body coming into him, warm-close and full. The tears were running now, racing the hollows of the shadowed cheeks, choking the throaty catch of her voice. "My Ben," she sobbed. "My sweet, dumb, wonderful, big Ben! You're making me say it, boy. You're tearing it out of me—"

The slender arms tightened convulsively as she pulled herself swiftly up and into him.

"I love you, Ben. God forgive me, I love you—!"

Chapter Sixteen

THE BADLANDS of central Wyoming began in brooding earnest some miles south of old Fort Reno. For most of the remaining way the Bozeman Road skirted their fringe, being relatively level and open. Nearing Reno, however, the road veered sharply into them, the last fifteen miles below the fort being a trap of crossridges and timbered hills of considerable elevation.

It was this country into which Ben nervously eased the herd at five o'clock the morning of October 15.

Nothing happened.

By noonhalt they had seen no hostile sign whatever. The only things silhouetting the crowded hills were the stunted yellow pine and native hemlock of the region. The sole alien force sweeping down from them upon the restless Texas herd, was the lonely sough and whistle of the autumn wind.

With the cattle back on trail at two o'clock, moving briskly with the smell of water ahead and with Reno and the Powder River but eight miles, four hours, ahead, Ben eased back in the saddle. For once Stark had been right. Apparently they did indeed have the herd too close to the military for Sioux comfort.

The scouts at Laramie had done their best for Ben in the few hours the big Texan was available to them. But you don't teach the more delicate shadings of Sioux culture in a few hours, regardless how hard the student listens. Ben's Indian education left off a little short of Fort Reno, Wyoming Territory.

About four miles short, to be exact.

At precisely 3.30 P.M. by Nathan Stark's fine gold pocket watch.

There was no warning.

No orthodox gathering atop the nearest hill, to form a line of painted ponies and eagle feather war bonnets.

No accepted protocol of hurled insults and dire predictions of the brief and bloody shrift facing the rash white brother, ahead of the warwhooping charge.

And, in fact, not even any warwhoops to begin with.

One minute the herd was passing peacefully around the precipitous flank of a curving, timberless ridge. The next second a silent, crouched double horde of ocher-smeared tribesmen was bombarding its unshod ponies over the southern shank of the ridge and down onto the straggling drag.

Perhaps "horde," historically, was an overstatement. It only seemed like one to the startled cowboys hazing the drag. They could see nothing but herd dust, stampeding cattle, flashes of piebald horsehide, the bob and whip of feather headdresses and, now that they were full into the herd, the harshly screaming faces of the hostile riders.

Actually, there were only about fifty of them. But to the dumbfounded cowboys of the drag, four in number, under the dour chaperonage of old Chickasaw Billings, they seemed like fifteen hundred.

Technically, they may as well have been. The Indian never sends a papoose to do a brave's work. These dark-skinned Wyoming missionaries were long years off the cradleboard. They did their work quickly and with honest pride.

Three thousand cattle on drive, no matter you're nervous and have them bunched as close as they will walk, cover a lot of trail. Ben, riding point with Clint and Stark, was a full mile north of the point of ambush and well out of sight of it around the bend in the ridge, when the distant shrill of the first war cries stood his ash-blond hair on end.

By the time he raced his black clear of the ridge and could see what was happening, it was no longer happening.

The hollow boom of the Indian trade muskets and the staccato bicker of the cowboy Colts died as suddenly as it had started. He could see only the dust hanging over the rear of the herd. In the time it took him to gallop the black back along the bawling cattle, picking up the eight swing riders on the way, that dust had begun to lift and he could see a little more. Enough, at least, to let him see what was under it.

And what was under that dust was—nothing.

The drag was gone.

He slid the black to a stop, legging off of him and running to where Chickasaw crouched over the two white men on the ground. He was in time to get the old cowboy's dry-cursed story, and to verify it with his own squinting glance along the southern spur of the ridge.

Just disappearing over that ridge at stampeded tilt, howled on their way by the wheeling red riders behind them, were the two or three hundred cattle of the drag.

The two cowboys stretched in the trail were not dangerously wounded, but they would never see Montana that fall. One had an arrow through his left side, low down and in the flesh and missing the bowel, but driven clear through. The other had taken a smoothbore musket ball where it hurt his dignity as a worthy son of Texas more than it endangered his immediate future among the living.

It was Clint's hard-grinned guarantee that he wouldn't "likely set a saddle in any notable degree of comfort till the grass turned green agin."

Stark, even amid the uproar, holding bluntly to business as usual, insisted the first duty lay with the injured riders. Ben, sparing a quick look at the degree and nature of their wounds, and exchanging dry Texas diagnoses with their indignant sufferers, allowed they wouldn't die short of sundown and, with the entire cursing agreement of the stricken twain, reckoned the prime responsibility lay with the missing cattle.

Stark at once bucked him. When he did, western good humor in the face of adversity lost its earthy salt and turned alkali.

"By God," said Ben slowly, "you go ahead and squander your time ridin' to the fort and fetchin' back your army ambulance. These boys ain't goin' to expire, less'n it's from shame. But happen we don't git them cattle back and stomp them damn redguts into the dirt, expirin' is apt to git wholesale hereabouts. You onct leave a Injun run over you, he'll stampede you silly, you hear me?"

"Ben!"

Stark jumped it at him, bulldog jaw outthrust.

"I don't want any pursuit of those Indians. I say it's a trick to draw us away from the trail. Let them have the cattle, we can spare them. We'll drive on right now. That's an order, Ben."

"Why, yes sir," said Ben soberly. "I'll take thet order jest as soon's I git back, too. You see iffen I don't."

He broke away from Stark, wheeled on the gathering cowboys.

"Chickasaw, Waco, Hogjaw, Slim, Charley—you go along with Clint and me. The rest of you git back around the herd. Hold it right where it damn stands. Bunch the wagons and make these two heroes comfortable. Mr. Stark—" he spun back to the Virginia Citian—"you give my regards to Major Whoozis at Fort Reno. And git the goddam hell out'n my way."

He took the black from Clint, who had been holding him, swung up and kicked him into a gallop. He did not look back at the men he had named. The five stared after him a minute, ran for their reins-trailing ponies. Boarding them on the fly,

they slapped the Petmakers home, bunched in a sod-shower
ing gallop on Ben's rear. Their surprise wasn't anchored i
the gangling trailboss's all-out hurry, but in his unexpected
back-to-the-wagons direction. Chickasaw voiced their com
pany confusion the minute he could spur his rawboned gra
alongside Ben's big black.

"Whut in the name o' Christ you aimin' to do, Ben
Change inter a goddam pink coat and set o' lilywhite draws
and mebbe set out a dish o' blighty tea 'fore we up and dash
off arter the friggin' fox?"

"Suthin' like thet," grinned Ben.

The weathered Chickasaw had noticed that the time thes
Allison boys went to grinning on you was along about th
stretch most others would be weeping themselves red-eyed
Especially this damn, sobersided, six-and-a-half foot Ben
who never seemed to smile unless it was raining and the her
washing away down the river.

"Sech as suthin' like what?" he shouted sourly.

"Foxes," waved Ben. "Them's tolerable big ones, I reckon
And a right sizable pack of 'em. I ain't aimin' to run 'en
down with Sam Colts and slow-loadin' muzzleguns."

Chickasaw peered at him. Most of the boys carried Colt
only. The few who packed saddleguns had either old Civi
War carbines or even older, whipstick muzzleloaders. "Hell!"
he snorted. "They's only fifty o' the bastards!"

Ben slid the black up to the lead wagon. "Save you
breath, oldtimer," he laughed. "Gimme a hand with thes
here boxes."

It was the first time Chickasaw or any of the boys had seer
the five big packing boxes. Even Clint was getting his firs
eyeful of them.

But in a land where a man's best friend is his gun, and hi
next best, his horse, and dogs didn't even come close to it, th
stenciled legend along the narrow sides of the five boxes wa
in a language they could read as clear as the click of a Col
hammer. "THE REMINGTON ARMS COMPANY, IL
LION FORGE, N. Y." was a tongue understood an
accepted in the West, second only after that of "COLT PAT
ENT FIREARMS COMPANY, HARTFORD, CONN."

It was seven o'clock and full dark when Ben first caugh
the telltale red stain against the night sky off to their lef
"Jest like I thought," he grunted to Clint. "They didn't allov
they'd be shagged."

"Yeah," nodded Clint. "I bet they ain't bin really slappe

down since the damn army let 'em bluff it inter closin' the Bozeman. You know what thet blunthead, Stark, told me, Ben?"

"How's thet?"

"That goddam Carrington's got six hundred men up to Kearney and another two hundred down to Reno. Kin you imagine thet many whites knucklin' to two, three thousand Injuns?"

"Well," grinned Ben, "there's herd-run whites, and then there's Texicans."

"You jest said a mansize mouthful," laughed Clint. "Leave us git on along and live up to it."

"At the same time," broke in Waco Fentriss acidly, "leave us remember the dear, sainted Alamo."

"Yeah," breathed Charley Stringer uneasily. "Even Texicans kin be outnumbered."

"Bushway!" growled Chickasaw, sticking manfully to his earlier estimate. "They's no more'n fifty o' the bastards."

"Agin seven," drawled Ben, reining the black westward, toward the fire's glow. "And a box of Remin'ton Rollin' Block rifles."

"They shore load like a dream," was Hogjaw's irrelevant comment. With it, he headed the others after Ben and Clint, pushing his horse forward into the darkness.

Twenty minutes later, the seven cowponies were standing, reins trailing, in a slash of pine fifty feet below the skyline of the last ridge. And their baker's half-dozen bow-legged riders were bellied down in the pine needles and rimrock of its crest.

Below them, sharp and clear against the spark and boom of a victory fire, not seventy-five yards away and with their red paunches sleepily swollen with good Texas beef, squatted thirty Sioux braves.

The missing twenty-or-so of their fellows were undoubtedly bedded down and sleeping off the gastronomic fruits of heavy Oglala industry. In any event, what time Ben and his companions felt they had at their disposal was not squandered in guessing games as to the whereabouts of the missing score of red celebrants, but in laying a calm Texas eye down the barrel of a new Remington rifle onto the thirty victors then present—and soon to be accounted for.

Even in the dark, the new rifles loaded delightfully.

"Son of a bitch!" shouted Waco, flipping the falling block

back and dropping in his third shell. "They go in like antelope tallow to a dry hub!"

"You ain't jest whistlin' Dixie!" chortled old Chickasaw, one up on Waco and slamming his fourth round, closed "And, mister, do they hold tight! Watch thet bastard runnin' to the left, yonder—"

Waco, presently drilling his third Sioux out of the yelling mill of startled redmen below, had neither time nor inclination to observe Chickasaw's called shot. Had he, he would have seen the thirteenth Sioux grab his belly and bounce into the sagebrush.

It was that wild and that short, from start to finish.

Within five minutes after the firing broke out along the darkened ridge, there wasn't an Indian within buffalo-gun range of the stolen herd below.

Having but one way to estimate the numbers of their attackers—by the rapidity of their fire—the Sioux could only assume there were at least two dozen white riflemen along the ridge. These were not odds to the Oglala liking, and an every-redman-for-himself exit was in instant order.

Ben and his triumphant Texans had only to blow out the hot barrels of their new guns, amble down and board their ponies, put them over the ridge and into the level draw beyond, leisurely collect their borrowed cattle and head for home.

Well, there were one or two other little things.

Of the thirteen braves seen to drop, they could find but five. They were left to figure that the hostiles, as they always did when sheer guts and superb horsemanship could bring it off, had somehow gotten the other eight aboard ponies and carried them off. The "one or two other little things" came in when it was discovered that two of the braves left behind were still alive.

Chickasaw did the honors, with a hand well trained in such basic courtesies from thirty years, and more, of life beyond the fringe of white settlement life in West Texas.

When Ben ordered him out and away, to join the other boys with the cattle, himself lingering behind to kick out the fire, all five of the red brothers were long past pain: the final two of them staring peacefully up at the Wyoming stars around a powder-burned hole between the eyes.

Chapter Seventeen

THEY LOST ANOTHER three days at Fort Reno while Stark fretted over the advice of his friend Major Randall, Randall's opinion was that of Colonel Lamine at Laramie, ominously compounded.

Lamine had given them a slight chance, Randall gave them none.

He did, however, give them tacit permission to move on to Fort Kearney. It was first suggested by him and agreed to by Stark that a courier be sent to Kearney seeking Carrington's clearance to that point. Ben, sensing a risk in this, argued weather with Stark. It was October 18. They could not chance an hour's delay. It was the fractional uncertainty of the Sioux against the dead-zero sureness of a deep snow.

Stark, looking at the herd and seeing thirty-five dollars every time he saw a fat steer, folded. He went back to Randall and put the pressure on.

The old army game already had a long beard in 1866. You played it no differently, using the same weary buck and tired pass thereof. Nathan Stark was a big man; a political power in the territory with friends up to the rank of major general strung through the chain of command from Leavenworth to the Powder and beyond to Carrington himself.

The herd moved out for Fort Phil Kearney and Colonel Henry Carrington.

But after a long night of trying to sleep with his unauthorized decision, the good major wrote a covering letter and dispatched it to Kearney. He had, reluctantly, the report stated, permitted a Mr. Nathan Stark of Virginia City, Montana, to pass a herd of three thousand mixed breeding and beef cattle with clearance to Fort Kearney on the basis of the fact that Colonel Lamine had cleared the herd up the Bozeman from Laramie and that his, Randall's, authority could not take precedence in the matter without written direction from Carrington. There had been, further, some concern of a personal friendship with the commander at Kearney brought forward by the Montana civilian. Major Randall expressed his regrets and respects and requested further orders.

The courier was an old hand and a wise one. He rode only by night, and a roundabout course. Result of this Sioux circumspection was that an infuriated Carrington received news of Stark's approach only when Ben had the herd sixty-two miles north of Reno and a short seven south of Kearney.

Further result was that the wary Texan, outriding his point by four miles, rode up over a saddleback rise in the trail three miles from the fort, squarely into Company F, Troop C, Second United States Cavalry, Captain William J. Fetterman, Commanding.

Fetterman was a career officer, very impressed with his two silver bars, his unrecognized genius as a cavalry tactician, and his oft expressed disdain of the red brother. It had been his repeated boast that with fifty troops he could ride through the entire Sioux Nation. Accordingly, a simple company should be ample to halt three thousand cattle and thirty cowboys.

As a matter of record, it was.

Ben received Fetterman's version of his superior's ultimatum, along with the unauthorized sneer which came with it, calmly enough. A man had eyes, he had ears, he had, anyway, a part of a brain. There was the pompous little redhaired captain. There were his twenty nervous, green troopers. There were Colonel Henry B. Carrington's angry orders. A man could take them or leave them.

Ben compromised.

He took the orders, left Captain Fetterman and his downfaced boys in blue.

But when, twenty minutes later, he galloped into Stark and the head of the herd, he was anything but calm. "We're up agin another blockade," he rasped. "This un ain't goin to be no run-around like the Jayhawkers."

"You've seen Carrington!" ejaculated Stark, thinking he had been to the fort and back.

"Naw, a sawed-off captain named Fetterman. He's the colonel's boy, howsomever. Brought us a billydoo from headquarters, likewise."

"Well, man, what is it?" Stark scowled. "Don't tell me they're not going to let us through?"

"It ain't mine to tell you nothin', savin' what Fetterman told me. You kin take it from there, and to Carrington, I allow."

"Go on, for God's sake."

"We been give a quarantine line three mile south of the fort. Colonel needs the grass past that point fer his own stock. We ain't to set a heifer's hoof acrost thet line."

The herd was held up at once, thrown off the trail and onto graze. Stark departed for the fort. He was back by

106

nightfall and, as Clint soberly put it, "You could see the dust from his cussed tail a'draggin' a mile off."

Fetterman hadn't told them the half of it.

And Stark, ahead of that, in reporting the number of troops Carrington had at Kearney, had told them twice too much.

In the half-finished stockade ahead were less than three hundred men, a good part of them civilian packers and supply troops. Of regular troops, and most of them grass-green replacements, there were not over two hundred. Any question of a military escort up the Bozeman was grimly out. The order to halt the herd and not move it a stray head north of the three-mile line was official. And friendship or no friendship between him and Nathan Stark, Carrington would not hesitate to use his two hundred troops to enforce it.

Now they all knew where they stood.

In the middle of Wyoming, with winter coming on.

This time Stark took no vote. The grass and water were excellent where they were. There was good shelter from the high hills to the north, east and west. There was plenty of sizable timber within short hauling distance. And there were two hundred U.S. troops standing official guard only three miles away.

The Montanan continued to make his hard points as the cowboys gathered to listen in nodding silence.

They still had from three weeks to a month of open weather, barring a squaw winter. Lodgepole pine for corral rails stood by the slim thousand along the near hills. Heavier timber for sod huts and shelter sheds stood mixed in with it. By hard work and careful herding they could hope to winter through with reasonable losses. Then, with spring, they could backtrack, going over South Pass as originally suggested by Stark.

Clint, scowling at the stress on the last point, knew exactly what Stark meant.

The big slicker was going over Ben's head again, getting to the men, putting the blame on his trailboss, saving none of it for himself. Again, he would have braced the Montanan on the spot, but once more Ben interceded, defending Stark. Before the call for fair play was decently out of Ben's mouth, Stark was concluding his rationalization with the customary deft touch. With that touch, to Clint's cynical satisfaction, he proved three points.

To Stark's kind the end gain was everything. He was a considerable man, hard and tough as they came. He was a pretty square man, too, for the most part. But then, for the most part, he could afford to be. It's not hard to be easy on the whip when you've got a six-horse hitch on a downhill drag. But when you hit the steep spots, when your wheelers start to lay down on you, your swing team won't pull and your leaders will neither gee nor haw, look out.

Stark had set out to bring a herd of longhorns from Texas to Montana. If, in that process, he had to cut the guts out of Ben Allison, or anybody else, you could consider those guts cut.

He could have made his winter camp without blaming Ben for it. That wasn't his way. Stark was a leader of men, not a brother to them. When a mistake was made, the charge had to be put to somebody else's account. Otherwise, the leader might fall. In the present case, if Ben were left blameless the men might rally to him and his views instead of Stark and his. They had done so twice before. The Montanan's cold-deck credo, money before morals and the hell with who got hurt, simply demanded they be given no third chance. The knife came out and Ben got cut.

That was point one.

Point two was that Clint understood point one.

Point three was that Ben didn't.

For two days Ben worked the crew, getting up the main holding corral for the beef stock and a second, smaller enclosure for the draft and riding stuff. Twenty-four-hour guard-shifts were run. There was, ominously, no interference from the Indians. And this despite the fact that a big band of hostile scouts had hung off their flanks all the way up from Fort Reno.

On the morning of the 21st, with the corrals completed and the stock safely in them, Ben rode to Fort Kearney. He was gone all day but when he rode in after dark that night he had the answer to what had been bothering him—where were the Sioux all the time they were throwing up those corrals?

The simple answer—the Sioux had been busy.

He got his information from the same source he had used at Laramie; the post's enlisted and civilian scouts. His prime informant this time was one Pawnee Perez, variously known as Portugee Phillips and Wyoming John, a halfbreed civilian scout born among and reared by the Oglala Sioux.

Perez had just come in off a scout into the Wolf Mountains and along the Tongue River north of the fort. On the Tongue he had found a warcamp of eight hundred lodges. By frontier rule-of-red-thumb, two warriors to a lodge, this added up to at least fifteen hundred braves in that one camp, alone. He had seen two other, smaller camps of about one hundred fifty lodges, each. And in the week he had been gone, no less than five hundred Indians were in daily operation around the fort itself.

And not wasting their time.

In the three days since Fetterman had halted the herd, Carrington had lost twenty men out of three wood-cutting and hay-hauling parties outside the fort, and had had every last head of saddlestock, saving Fetterman's forty troop horses, run off by the constantly raiding and retreating redmen. Other than Fetterman's few mounts and perhaps eight or ten hitches of wagon mules, the Colonel's own Kentucky thoroughbred was the sole saddle animal left to the Kearney command.

And more.

Constantly harassed and piecemeal butchered by the sharpshooting Sioux, the wood and hay details had not been able to get in enough of either fodder or fuel to carry the garrison through December.

Carrington's two hundred infantry would be lucky to finish the fort before Crazy Horse's five hundred advance cavalry finished its builders. And the red commander had two thousand reserves squatting along the Tongue not thirty miles north!

It was Pawnee Perez's opinion, grimly returned to Stark & Company by its worried trailboss, that with the fort now cauterized and sewn off, the Sioux would turn their leisure attention to the three thousand spotted buffalo and thirty Ride-A-Heaps below that fort.

The liberal Indian education of the Texas cowboys and their Montana herd owner had by this time progressed to the point where their knowledge of the colorful Sioux patois was amply sufficient to allow them to translate Ben's use of Perez's vernacular into no uncertain personal terms.

The silent riders looked first at Stark, then at one another. Not a man bothered to put words to the obvious.

To the Sioux, the multi-colored Texas longhorns were simply "spotted buffalo."

Accepting this Oglala definition of the cattle, the dullest witted of their big-hatted chaperons encountered no difficulty guessing who the "Ride-A-Heaps" might be.

Spell it any way you wanted—Sioux, Sedalia, Laramie, Reno, Fort Worth or West Texas—you didn't pronounce it any different. The accent was on the "C" and the second syllable was "scared." Put it all together, it came out one word. Cowboy.

That was you, mister!

Chapter Eighteen

AN HOUR AFTER Ben made his report, the herd camp returned to an uneasy quiet. What riders were not on herd guard or picket duty remained around the chuckwagon fire, Saleratus McGivern, for once forgetting to complain about it, kept the coffee kettle constantly replenished, taking time out only for repeated nervous checks beneath his floursack apron to make sure his ancient Walker Colt was still stuck in the waistband of his Levis, ready, there, for commissary duty not concerned with the baking of biscuits or the brewing of mocha beans.

Ten o'clock passed, and eleven. Still no man sought his blankets. If they were waiting for something without knowing exactly what, their uncertainty was soon resolved.

Nathan Stark pulled out his engraved pocket watch for the third time in ten minutes. "Nearly midnight," he said to Ben. Then, to the waiting riders, "You boys better catch-up. You go out in five minutes."

The cowboys nodded, drifting away from the fire in twos and threes, moving for the saddled night horses picketed around the woodwagon's tailgate. The first of them was stepping up on his mount when the sound of drumming pony hoofs checked his swing-up.

The approaching rider slid his horse into the firelight and stepped down. It was Slim Blanchard.

"What's up, Slim?" said Ben quickly. "Where's the Kid?"

The Kid was Curly Blanchard, Slim's nephew, a pleasant drawling youth of eighteen, youngest rider in the crew and by all odds the apple of its hardbitten eye.

"It's whut I dunno," said Slim tersely. "We was ridin' the main corral gate, him north, me south. I passed him five minutes ago and all was quiet. Jest arter he'd gone by I heered some kind o' scuffle back over ahint me. I doubled back and bumped inter the Kid's hoss in the dark. They wasn't nobody on him."

"Let's go," said Ben, and ran for the black.

They found Curly thirty yards from the corral fence. They hadn't had time to scalp him or cut him up. There was only one mark on him and the Sioux skinning knife that made it was still sticking in it—from behind.

"I reckon," said Ben, "we ain't time fer no formal services."

"I'll fetch a wagon tarp," said Waco Fentriss.

Slim Blanchard said nothing, and was joined in it by the remaining trap-jawed dozen of his fellow Texans.

They got the boy into the tarp, back to the fire.

"Where'll we put him, Ben?" asked Slim, dry-eyed.

"In the lead wagon."

"They ain't room," muttered the tall cowboy.

"There will be," said Ben. "Waco, Chickasaw—Heave the rest of them Remin'ton boxes out'n there. Hogjaw, you and Charley knock 'em open. Save the wood. Mr. Stark, you and Saleratus strip them rifles. Git the grease out'n their barrels and rack 'em up here alongside the chuckwagon. The rest of you git on out to the herd. Tell them other boys to hump their butts back in here."

As the cowboys began legging-up, Ben stepped to the stirrup fenders of a darkbearded rider from Fort Worth. "Tex," he nodded, "take two boys and snake yer ropes onto them first three lineposts on the north side. Pull out that fence and git them cattle on the trail."

"She's pulled," said Tex Anderson.

"Clint's on guard over to the workstock corral," added Ben. "Send a boy fer him and have him take over the herd. Tell him Stark'll pay him overtime, past midnight." The grin which flashed behind the last comment would not have been recognized as such unless a man was familiar with what might strike a quarter-blood Comanche as funny.

The cowboys were already fading into the darkness before Nathan Stark caught up with Ben's timed-fire directions. He had only time to digest the idea of his herd being thrown on the trail in the middle of the night and in the heart of Sioux country, and to get the first three words of objection out of his startled mouth, when Ben cut into him colder than an ice saw.

"Mr. Stark," said the Texan, stepping into him and holding his voice down for Montana ears alone, "you'd best git the far hell out'n my way. You want to stay here and winter through by yerse'f, you jest do it. I don't aim to stand by and see our boys knocked off one-by-one. Me and the herd's movin' on."

Nathan Stark stood back. By this time he knew the Texas tempers. He saw the look on Ben's face. He had seen the look on young Curly's. And the looks on the hard faces of his fellow cowboys when they brought the dead boy in. If ever on the fifteen hundred long miles from Fort Worth there had been a time for following the drag and keeping well back out of the dust, that time was right now.

Stark knew that. And with the exercise of his monumental control, he once more held his hand.

He looked past the fire and past the darkness beyond it. He saw his three thousand steers and six wagonloads of supplies going up in the warsmoke that waited along the Tongue River beyond Fort Kearney. Still, he knew he could not stop Ben and the Texans tonight. A man could only guess what lay in the big trailboss's mind. But he didn't have to guess too hard. The uncrating and stripping of the Remingtons could mean but one thing. Ben intended to outflank Fort Kearney and Carrington's absolute orders, to take himself and Stark and their low-voiced argument past the chance of the colonel's interference, and to gamble his guts and thirty Rolling Block rifles against Crazy Horse and three thousand Indians.

It was a hard commentary on Nathan Stark's own quota of courage that his reply to Ben Allison's blunt warning was an even blunter one of his own.

"Ben," he said quietly, "this time you've gone too far."

"Not half so far," answered Ben, pale-eyed, "as I aim to go."

"All right," nodded Stark. "It's your saddle. Ride it the way you see it."

"She's rode," said Ben, and went for the black gelding.

They traveled far that night. In the five hours before the false dawn they pushed the cattle ten miles beyond the fort. And in the two hours remaining before full daylight they forced them another five.

Behind them, in the cold October darkness, lay Big Piney Creek, Squaw Pine Ridge, Peno Creek Bottoms. Beyond them lay the grass-grown ruts of the abandoned Bozeman Road. And beyond the road waited the distant Tongue; beyond it, again, the yet more distant Big Horn.

They could not know the names—Big Piney, Squaw Pine, Peno Bottoms. They passed them swiftly in the frosty starlight. Yet within two months those names would be known to them and to all western men. But Captain Theodore Ten Eyck was still sixty days from gazing horror-stricken from the heights of Squaw Pine Ridge, down across the brooding silence of the Peno Bottoms and the frozen bodies of Captain William J. Fetterman and his eighty mutilated men. And the two thousand Sioux who would stream up at Ten Eyck from

113

the bloodied forks of the Peno, driving him back to Kearney with the ghastly news of the Fetterman Massacre, were still in their fire-banked tipis along the Tongue.

When Ben and his Texans passed that grim way in the early morning hours of October 22, only the far-off call of a hunting wolf and the nearby mutter of the nightwind in the stunted timber disturbed the eerie quiet of Squaw Pine Ridge.

The herd was put on tightly guarded graze at seven o'clock. The weary crew gathered at the chuckwagon while Saleratus stirred a bag of Arbuckle's into the coffee kettle and turned the smoking steaks in their tubsized frying pans. Ben let the men eat first, then, with the third tins of mocha poured and the oilskin pouches of longleaf Burley coming out, he put it to them.

"Boys," he shrugged, "it's jest as simple as you seen it worked last night. Every night we drive. Every day we hold up and keep the wagons circled. An Injun dearly hates the dark and he don't know how to fight in it, ceptin' to sneak in and cut singles out'n the herd like they done with Curly. Beyond thet, iffen we drive hard by night and watch out sharp by day, I allow we kin make it through."

He paused and when none of them spoke, went on.

"The other way was what we was doin' down yonder. Settin' and waitin' for 'em to carve us off, one-by-one. With all winter to do the carvin' I reckon you don't need no diagrams to figger the shape they'd have our rumps cut into by spring."

"I reckon," nodded old Chickasaw Billings, "that we one and all kin see where we was last night. Ain't nobody got no argiments with thet, Ben. Question is, boy, where are we this mornin'?"

"Right where you want to be, or where you say you are," grunted Ben. "My say is this here road and Montany. Mr. Stark's is thet there winter camp and Fort Kearney."

Again he paused and again the men waited.

"Speakin' of Mr. Stark," he went on slowly, "I got suthin' I want got straight by all of you. He's treated me and all of us fair and square. The way he sees the Sioux it made sense to go inter thet camp below Kearney and wait 'em out. The way I see 'em, it don't. There ain't no more to it than thet. I ain't buckin' him on who the cattle belongs to, nor on who's payin' yer wages. I've tooken his orders right along and I mean to take 'em yet—providin'."

He stopped short on the last word and Stark, listening carefully as he had gone along, watching the men and their reactions as he always did, now only nodded calmly and

114

asked. "Providing what, Ben?" He was playing it safe again, passing the raise, wanting to know for sure where the men stood before upping the ante.

"Providin' thet from here on you stick to yer set of trace chains and don't step over mine."

"Make sense, man."

"You handle the money, leave me point the cattle."

"I'd say that was up to the men, wouldn't you?"

"It ain't up to the cows," said Ben. "Let's git on with it."

"I reckon there ain't no call to git very fur——"

It was old Chickasaw Billings again, stepping forward and facing his fellow riders.

"One vote fer Ben Allison and Virginy City."

"Second the motion," said Waco, coming up off his heels and lounging to Chickasaw's side. "All them not in favor signify by raisin' yer right hand"—he underlined it with a soft pat of his worn holster—"*with a Colt in it.*"

"I allow I kin outdraw ye, Waco," drawled Hogjaw Bivins. "But not on thet proposition. Three votes fer Little Benjamin and his mother-friggin' Bozeman Road."

"Four," added Slim Blanchard. "And one fer Curly makes five."

"Six," corrected Charley Stringer. "The returns from Uvalde County jest come in."

"All any o' you bastards know how to do is eat," growled Saleratus McGivern. "You none of you never learnt to count. Seven."

"Eight," amended the spade-bearded Tex Anderson. "And damn if the polls didn't jest close."

One of the cowboys, a youngster from John Bell Hood's Texas Brigade and a war comrade of Clint's, grinned easily. "Fair enough, Tex. We-all will mark our ballots and send 'em back from Montany. Three cheers fer the Confed'racy!"

One of the bowlegged constituency cut loose from the back row with an ear-piercing Rebel yell. It was picked up and improved upon by twenty-odd loyal Texas throats and old Chickasaw broke up the meeting with six shots through the canvas spine of the woodwagon and a thigh-slapped "P'int 'em north by Gawd! And six bits reeward fer the fust Sioux sca'plock plucked barehanded!"

None of the suddenly rejuvenated cowboys had noticed Clint Allison standing back from the fire, failing to take part in the vote.

They noticed him now. Him and his flat, soft voice. And his faraway, vacant leer.

"Sorry to bring you the bad news from the west, boys," he sneered uglily. "But San Saba, Texas, jest seceded from the Union."

Wheeling on him, Ben's pale eyes narrowed.

You knew Clint, you knew that damn-nasty, slit-eyed sneer. And where it came from.

Somewhere, somehow, between midnight and daybreak, Clint had found a bottle.

He was dead drunk.

The stillness held. Clint steadied himself against the wood wagon, Ben stood facing him, feet spread, arms hanging loosely. None of the others moved or spoke.

Clint was a dangerous-when-wet proposition. Enough of the watching men had found that out in the bistros of Old Fort Worth before starting the drive. Those who hadn't took their first look at him now, and didn't need to be told to stand back and stay wide. On the frontier you learned young to read roadbrand and earmarks on a bad drunk.

"Clint," said Ben gently, "you crazy or suthin'?"

Clint laughed, and it was not a pleasant sound. "I may be suthin'," he said hoarsely. "But I ain't crazy. *You* are, big brother!"

"What're you sayin', boy?"

"Jest this," growled Clint. He was not laughing nor loose-grinning anymore. "I'm peed so full of you and Stark and the dumbhead way you're lettin' him play you thet my back teeth are floatin'."

"Clint—!"

"Shet up, Ben. I'm gonna say it. You're gonna hear it."

"Keep talkin', son," said Ben soothingly. "I'm listenin'."

"Stark'll git to you, Ben." Clint seemed to sober in one of those wide-eyed, fleeting seconds of lucidity a very drunk man will show. "He'll do it and you'll never feel it goin' inter you. Watch the son of uh bitch, you hear me, Ben—*watch him!*"

"Clint, boy." Ben said it softly, pointing the course of the small stream along which the herd was being grazed. "Yonder's a stretch of cottonwood. Hunt yerse'f some shade and sleep it off. You're talkin' wild."

"Ben—" The smile faded back, quick, loose. The staring look of the intense blue eyes grew dark, steadied uncertainly on Ben. "I'm comin' off this wagon. Don't be in my way."

Ben was standing very close to him. He didn't move. "Where'd you git the whiskey, Clint?" he said quietly.

"Git out'n my way—"

Ben stepped into him. He seized him, blocking his right arm with his hip, twisting him back against the wagon. "Where'd you git it!" he snarled. "Goddam you, Clint Allison, don't put off on me!"

Clint didn't move. His dark face writhed, turned strangely pale. The hushed men scarcely heard his harsh whisper. *"Ben! Git your hands off'n me!"*

Ben knew he should not have touched him. Knew the Comanche craziness that got into him when he was drunk and anybody laid hands on him. But this. This miserable, bastardly luck. To have beaten the south plains rains, the Jayhawk blockade, the hell's heat of the Platte Valley, the Sioux raid at Reno, Carrington and his three-mile line—the whole lousy fifteen hundred miles of it—for what? This, for God's sake? To end up with Clint drunk and Crazy Horse waiting over the next ridge? With three hundred miles and two thousand Sioux ahead of you, and your righthand gun so slobbered he couldn't stand up without a wagon behind him!

Ben took his hands away. He touched him lightly on the shoulder, stepped slowly and carefully back. "I'm sorry, boy," he murmured. "I reckon I never figgered you'd fold on me." Then, still quiet but with the flint back in it. "Where'd you git the whiskey, Clint?"

He got his answer from Nathan Stark, moving belatedly forward, his pink face flushed.

"Ben, it's my fault. He must have seen me putting it with my things in the lead wagon. It was a quart of Kentucky Blend. I got it from Fetterman at the fort. He insisted I take it, and—"

"Then goddam *you*," said Ben through his teeth. "Don't you know no better than to leave whiskey where an Injun kin get at it!" He didn't say it funny. Nobody took it that way.

He turned to Clint.

"What're you meanin' to do, boy? Pull out?"

"And far out!" muttered Clint thickly. "I hired on as a wetnurse fer you and yer crazy scheme. Where you're headin' now you won't need nothin' but a undertaker and that's out'n my line. Move back, damn you, Ben. Quit inchin' up on me. I mean it!"

"I won't stop you, boy," said Ben. "But we're almost to Montany, son. Nigh to the Gallatin. She's jest acrost the Yellerstone yonder, Clint. Don't chuck her, now—"

"You're stallin', Ben." The laugh was there again, short, wild. "Brains ain't yer play, not never. Leave 'em to yer lousy

117

friend yonder." He jerked a big thumb at Stark. "But don't worry about little Clint—goddam you, Ben, stay where you are!"

Ben stopped. He felt his belly pull in. He knew he had pushed him as far as any man could. Knew he was not going to get in close enough to grab him again. Knew that he would have to go for him now, gun or no gun.

And Clint was watching him. Watching him with the blank stare of the professional gunman, and watching him, beyond the stare, with the ageless, dangerous cunning of the very drunk. In the last second, Ben hesitated. In that same second, Clint's Army Colt was out and in his hand. And in the next was pointing Ben's belly.

"One vote," snarled Clint, thick lipped, "fer Fort Kearney and Fetterman's footlocker."

He swung the sundance of the Colt barrel around the nervous ring of men beyond his brother.

"Any of you sons uh bitches want to contest it?"

Ben knew it was too late, then. He made no more move than the last tightfaced cowboy behind him.

"Stark!" Clint flicked the gunbarrel across Nathan Stark's beltbuckle. "You're the financial genius hereabouts. Git figgerin' my cut. And lemme fill yer flush—"

He stepped into the Montanan, jammed the Colt's muzzle hard into him. "Some of us Allisons ain't the unedicated bastards others is. This un learnt to count."

"Clint," said Stark, jaw set, "be reasonable. Do as Ben says. Go sleep it off. We'll forget the whole thing, you have my word on it."

"Now, me," continued the drunken youth, ignoring him with his heavily drawled conclusion, "I learnt to count clean up to ten. Yes suh, I kin do anythin' up to and includin' ten. Add, subtract, multiply—*and divide by three.*"

Stark turned away from him. "Ben," he said angrily, "what in God's name is he talking about? What does he want of me?"

Ben moved forward, away from the others. He dropped his voice, meaning it for Stark alone.

"He wants one third of ten thousand dollars," he said quietly. "Give it to him."

"Ben! By the Lord, I'll not do it!"

"I said give it to him. It's his and comin' to him. Write him a draft, you hear, Mr. Stark?"

"Ben, we can't turn him loose to go back to the fort. I don't care about the money, you know that. But we're only fifteen miles from Carrington. Suppose Clint starts drinking again back there and it gets out we've driven on? Fetterman's cavalry could catch us in six hours!"

"I allow I know that," said Ben. Then, with sudden slowness. "I thought *you* was the one all hot fer Fort Kearney, yerse'f. Mr. Stark."

"Nonsense! I'm with you and the men," replied Stark stoutly. "They want to go on, and that's all I ask. But you know we can't turn Clint loose on a drunk like this. Nor is there a man in the crew who wouldn't agree with me on that. You know that too."

Ben knew it for sure.

"Give him the draft," he repeated flatly.

Stark threw up his hands, spun on his heel, went angrily for the lead wagon. He got out his papers, wrote hurriedly.

"Gimme it," said Ben.

He took the draft, turned to Clint, waiting behind them with the Colt.

"Here's yer money, boy," he nodded soberly. "Don't spend it all in one place."

Clint grinned, reached carelessly for the note. Just as carelessly, Ben let go of it just before Clint's fingers closed on it. The draft fluttered, fell earthward. Involuntarily, Clint started to bend forward. He realized his mistake in the process of making it. He checked his reaching hand, threw his eyes and his Colt back up onto Ben.

Ben's own Colt flashed, the arc of its swinging barrel glittering in the sun.

There was the dull sound of steel on bone. Clint followed the flutter of the fallen banknote, soundlessly into the dust of the Bozeman Road.

Chickasaw and Waco ran forward, the others crowding behind them. At Ben's nod, they picked Clint up, headed with him toward the creek and the cottonwoods.

Ben slowly holstered the .44.

He reached down into the dust, retrieved the soiled draft, folded it carefully and tucked it away in his cowhide vest.

He looked at Nathan Stark.

"Clint never could hang on to his money," was all he said.

Chapter Nineteen

FOR THE SECOND TIME that day, the Texas cowboys bore an uncomplaining burden toward the cottonwoods. They worked quickly with the mattocks and spades, opening the rich earth of the creek's meadow. It was, in the words of the old song, "a narrow grave, just six-by three." And no loner prairie ever waited to receive "the pallid youth at close of day."

When they at last stood back from their labors, the sun angled low across the Bozemen, lighting the little grove with its last rose-red candle.

Ben nodded, and Waco and Chickasaw took up the crudely nailed box. They lowered it carefully, grimacing at the hollow sound of it going home in the shallow earth as they were forced to drop it the last few inches. The spongy clods rattled down, quickly obscuring the stenciled requiem legend staring up from the pine crating top of the rough box: *THE REMINGTON ARMS COMPANY, ILLION FORGE, N.Y.*

The dirt was soon shoveled in, the covering sod, painstakingly removed in the beginning, was tamped carefully back in original place. The excess earth was as swiftly carried away and consigned to the moving waters of the little stream.

Ben stooped slowly. He wedged the last of the rifle-box boards deep into the cairn of creek rocks headmarking the hidden grave. The prowling coyote could not read; the dead would rest in peace. And a man felt better, somehow, to mark the place and the memory with something beyond a pile of prairie stone.

They stood back, then, looking at Ben's marker.

After a moment, Waco awkwardly removed his dust-caked hat.

Hogjaw coughed and shifted his run-over bootheels.

Behind them, Chickasaw fumbled clumsily with his bandanna, first wiping his face with it, then blowing his nose.

"I reckon," said Slim, low voiced, "somebody ought to say a few words." He looked around the silent company of bearded and booted mourners. Hogjaw shifted his feet again, Waco fiddled with his battered hat. Chickasaw cleared his throat, thought better of it, shrugged helplessly, dropped his eyes guiltily under the waiting appeal of Slim's glance.

The cowboy turned in last hope toward the slim figure of

Nella Torneau, standing behind Ben in the shadow of the crowding cottonwoods. "Miss Nella——?"

"Thank you, Slim."

They all saw the little Bible, now, held to her breast beneath her pilgrim cloak, and only Ben was not surprised. He remembered now. Among the scattered, golden moments he and this wonderful girl had shared there had been his question about the little engraved carbine she had killed Crazy Horse's pony with at Timpas Creek. And her answer came back now. Her father had told her as a little girl: a girl's born in Texas she's got to carry two things all her life, and learn to use them—a rifle and a Bible.

He had seen her use the rifle, now it was the good book. She read from the Twenty-Third Psalm, voice low, violet-blue eyes downcast: *The Lord is my shepherd, I shall not want. He leadeth me to lie down in green pastures . .*

She finished, and Ben swallowed hard. He looked quickly away, squinting into the low sun. "I allow the herd had best be got moving," he said softly. They turned away, no further prayer offered, no added farewell finding spoken word. Shortly, the packing case board and its knife-cut remembrance was alone with the dying stir of the evening wind in the cottonwoods.

GEORGE FRANK BLANCHARD
OCT. 1866
Ride easy, Curly

By dawn and forced drive they were thirty-five miles north of Fort Kearney. Clint, disarmed and in the informal, embarrassed custody of Waco and Chickasaw, had ridden the night away fighting down the last of the whiskey quease in his churning belly. And fighting, too, to bring some sense of where he was, and why, into the throbbing ache of his head.

All through the long hours of following daylight, he kept to himself and to his thoughts of himself.

Then, at dusk, with the coyotes beginning to tune up and the men bunching the herd to move with full dark, he found Ben alone at the chuckwagon.

The latter had ridden in but minutes before, from a near daylong scout of the next fifteen miles ahead. He was presently putting down a cold steak and tin of lukewarm coffee, against the weary proposition of climbing back in the saddle to try and get a few hours sleep across the jolting cradle of a jogging horse's back.

"Howdy, Ben——"

"Pull yerse'f up a cup of java and set down, boy."

Clint poured a cup, squatted alongside his silent brother, staring, with him, into the smoking coals of Saleratus's supper fire.

"I reckon I been a damn fool, agin."

"Runs in the fam'ly, boy."

"I aim to make it up to you, Ben."

"Fergit it. You et?"

"Belly wouldn't hold down a hoss-shoe stake."

"Better eat, regardless."

" 'Druther talk, I reckon."

"Your deck. Deal 'em."

Clint nodded. He talked low and quiet. And there was nowhere in it a grin, or a laugh, or a dark, wild look.

"Ain't no use, I reckon, to say no more on Stark."

"I reckon not. We see him different, boy, that's all. You been set on callin' him since we h'isted his poke in thet Alder Gulch crickbottoms."

"I allow. I hate his smooth guts. It's mainly why I got to say where I've come to. I reckon you know there ain't no whiskey workin' in me now."

"I reckon. You still aim to pull out on me?"

"Not on you, Ben, for Christ's sake. You're the reason I *am* cuttin' my stick. All my goddam useless life I been friggin' up ev'rythin' you set yer hand to. I know what this here herd means to you and what store you set by the chanct you allow it'll give you to amount to suthin'. You and thet high-special gal you got yonder in thet lead wagon. She's really suthin', Ben. Like no gal I ever seen nor heered tell of. I purty near ruint it all fer you and her, yestidday. Happen I don't git out, I'll manage it yet, too."

"I'll chance it, boy. Saddle up and ride along with me tonight. Come mornin' we'll take another look at it."

"I reckon it'll be a tolerable fur look, Ben."

"You know I ain't smart, Clint. Don't riddle me."

"I'll be long gone up the trail by then."

"*Up* it, Clint?"

"And fur."

"Thought you was all fer Fort Kearney?"

"Thet was the whiskey talkin'."

"Likely," said Ben slowly. Then, frowning. "*Up* the trail is nothin' but Injuns."

"More or less whut I had in mind, old son."

Clint's grin was suddenly back home around the corners of his wide mouth.

"Meanin'?"

"Meanin' you jest rode in off yer last scout on point fer this herd. Beginnin' in five minutes, yer little brother takes over thet department."

"I reckon not," said Ben, shaking his head. "It ain't the job you kin ask another man to do fer you."

"Don't recall you askin' nobody," grinned Clint. "Goddam you, Ben, a man wants to be a hero, don't you put off on him, you hear? You ain't the only he-coon in the Allison fam'ly's holler tree."

Ben scowled, not saying anything for a long time. Finally, he nodded. "I reckon I tail yer drift. How'll you ride 'er?"

"Git on out tonight. Stay out, less'n I see suthin' worth ridin' back about. Thet way, yer point's bein' rode by a expert and me and yer fat-butt business partner is bein' kept out'n forty-four range of one another."

"I reckon you got a fair idee of whut's up there?" With the statement, Ben thumbed the thickening night to the north.

"Takes a Injun to skin one," shrugged Clint. "I reckon I'm a better Comanche than you'll ever be."

"Well," now it was Ben's rare smile softening the fire-light, "you *act* more like one anyways, you goddam Kwahadi slit-eye."

"Oh, bless you, noble white brother, fer yer straight tongue and yer big, thick head. I reckon I could never live with myse'f again, less'n I went ahead on and finished wetnursin' you inter the goddam Gallatin."

He got up, face relaxed now in the old, happy, wide-eyed half-smile. "Th'ow me some of thet cold beef inter a floursack whiles I kick thet haybelly sorrel of mine out'n thet Wyomin' buffler browse she's bogged in, yonder."

"Hold on," said Ben, coming to his feet in easy turn. He felt in his vest, brought out the crumpled wad of Stark's bankdraft. "You still want this?"

"Nope. Jest dig my Colts out'n yer duffle. You keep the draft. You kin give it to me over yonder where the Bozeman peters out." He waved into the northwest darkness, toward Montana and Virginia City. "Thet's where I'll be mainly needin' it, you kin lay. Me and thet hefty-chested blond heifer!"

"I hope so, Clint boy." Ben said it under his breath, and after his brother had turned lightheartedly away. "I sure and only hope so—"

The first attack came at the crossing of the Tongue. At this point in its high course, the stream was not large, but narrow and in spots deep, and over all possessed of considerable current. A night crossing became an unwarranted risk. Ben's decision, taken at four o'clock of a cloudy afternoon, was to put the herd on trail an hour early, try to time its crossing for the last hour of daylight.

It had been two days since Clint had ridden on up the trail. He had not returned and Ben, knowing his brother's ability to take care of himself in Indian country, had assumed he had found no Sioux sign ahead, had ridden on across the Tongue. He put the lead steers into the water at ten minutes after four.

At a quarter of five, with the gray daylight failing and eight hundred cattle still to be brought over, the Sioux struck.

They came in from the east bank, out of a low range of hills flanking the crossing to the northeast. There were about three hundred of them, picked warriors, Ben figured, from the compact way they rode and the absence of preliminary warning warwhoops. He was on the east bank with Waco, Charley Stringer and Chickasaw, circling and hazing the drag up and into the Tongue.

"Leave 'em!" he yelled to Chicksaw, nearest him. "Git acrost to the wagons! They ain't after cows this trip!"

Chickasaw waved, shouted the order on to Waco and Charley. "Ben says jump the river! Last one acrost's a baldheaded cowboy!" Baldheaded, his two companions assumed, by courtesy of a Sioux scalping knife, and lost no second digging their fresh night horses for the rocky channel of the Tongue.

On the far side, as Ben and his companions hit the water, Nathan Stark, taking over from the absent Clint as Ben's strawboss, already had the wagons going into a good circle. Ben noted that, only thinking to himself that Stark, though he might be somewhat less than he had figured him, was considerable more than Clint had. One thing was certain. The blond-bearded Montanan had guts enough to stuff two fouryear old steers, with a sizable handful left over to start on a third.

By the time he and the drag riders slid their mounts through the last gap in Stark's circle, the first of the Sioux were screaming their ponies across the Tongue. Seconds later some six or seven of them were still screaming—but not on their ponies. The Rolling Blocks spoke, and spoke again, and then spoke yet a third and a fourth and even a fifth time, before the last of the Sioux were well into the water.

With the addition of Waco's, Chickasaw's and Charley

Stringer's rifles, snatched on the bowlegged run from the tailgate of the lead wagon, there were twenty-five of the new Remingtons in breech-slamming action. With Ben's and Nella's sharp-barking little Henry carbines cracking over the deeper roar of the Rolling Blocks, it meant that a fire of nearly one hundred rounds per deafening half minute was getting into the charging warriors.

Red squaw had not yet groaned in smokestained cowhide tipi with the labor pains of the man-child who would make warrior enough to take that weight of lead and keep coming.

The Sioux split, right and left, up the west bank of the Tongue. They were gone back into the gathering dusk as swiftly, if less numerous by eight braves, as they had come out of it.

There were three crawlers among the eight downed Indians. The cursing cowboys killed them with riflefire from the wagons, not bothering to move in close and make it neat with handguns.

There was no time for such niceties. There had been three hundred of them and there might be three thousand more where that three hundred had come from. Miles were the idea right now. Herd miles, cowboyed and ropewhipped out of the milling cattle, as many of those miles and as far and long of them as might be driven under by first light.

In the last remaining twilight of the 25th of October, under the wagon-entrenched rifles of Stark and ten of the cowboys, Ben and the other fifteen riders put eight hundred cattle across the Tongue River in less than half an hour.

By six o'clock and full dark, the herd was moving due west for Montana and the southward sprawling forks of the Big Horn.

Jogging his black through the darkness a hundred feet ahead of the lead steers, Ben heard the light, quick chop of the approaching pony's singlefoot, knew without looking back who it was riding up on him. He knew everything about her—even the sound of her calico mare's sun-dancy way of going.

"Evenin', girl," he smiled. "How's the patient?"

The patient was old Chickasaw, who had taken a smoothbore Sioux ball through the crown of the two things he held most dear in life: his mildewed beaver hat, his proudly long thatch of bristly gray hair.

"It's the damn hat that's fretting him," laughed Nella. "He wouldn't let me touch his ornery old head till I'd dug out the sewing kit and run a new band around that verminy hat. He's

125

all right. Just a tolerable clean skull scratch. We'll never bury that old mossyback, but I'd purely admire to put that god-awful hat about six foot under. Ughh!"

Ben eased back in the saddle, reached over and sought in the darkness for her hand. "Good to hear you laugh agin, Nella. I reckon it's what keeps a man out in front of his cattle and squintin' the trail beyond."

She didn't answer for a minute, then asked softly, "What do you see out there, Ben?"

"What you mean?"

" 'Out there.' " she said, gesturing into the night. "In the beyond."

"Meanin' fer you and me?"

"For all of us, Ben. You, me, Clint, Stark, the whole mixup. What's out there?"

Ben knew she wasn't just talking. The way she asked it was too quiet, and of a sudden there wasn't anymore laugh in it.

"You're like Clint," he said slowly. "Deeper'n me, with yer talk. Allus meanin' suthin' you ain't sayin', and figgerin' I'm sharp enough to dig it out. I aint, Nella. You got to deal 'em face up fer me. Only mind I kin read is a cow's. And mebbe sometimes a man's—happen he's thinkin' me over with his hand hangin' close to his gun. Women run me a blind trail and allus have."

"I reckon they do, Ben," she answered softly. "And men, too, when they don't come at you with a gun."

"Meanin'?"

"Stark, Ben."

She was for sure like Clint, he thought. Trying to put him wise to Stark, thinking he couldn't see for himself, slow minded or not.

"Nella," he said at last, "Stark don't fool me too much, not like it looks, I allow. It's jest thet I see what he's after, like I've told you. Fer him nothin' counts but gittin' this herd inter thet Gallatin Valley. He'll likely do anythin' he thinks he's got to, to git 'em there. They ain't cows to him, not like they are to me, nor even Clint. They're money." He paused, nodding soberly. "And thet's all he's after, girl. It ain't like you and Clint think. He ain't after me."

"You missed me, Ben," she said softly. "I wasn't meanin' he was after *you*—"

There was a limit to any man's slowness. Ben's pale eyes narrowed. "By God, Nella," he growled hoarsely, "iffen he's layed a goddam—"

"No, no Ben," she interrupted quickly. "It's not that, boy.

He hasn't touched me. His kind never comes at anything they want with their hands. Don't you know that yet?"

"Mebbe," said Ben darkly. "How's he come at *you?*"

"Like he comes at everything," she answered bitterly. "With money and like it was a business deal. And like he could afford to pay more than anybody better dare turn down."

"Go on—"

"Ben, he's offered me half of Montana, with Alder Gulch and Virginia City throwed in. And he means it, Ben!"

"He means what?" said Ben thickly.

"To marry me."

She said it in a small voice, as if she knew it would hit him heavy—and she wanted to make it as light as possible. And as kind.

Stark was a rich man. He was going to be a lot richer. When he said half of Montana, he was only funning by probably five or six years of future. And he was a real man, too. Real in a way the likes of him and Clint could never be. Nathan Stark knew two things most men never learn till it's way too late—what he wanted and how to get it. He was a big man and a damn tall one. Alongside him and his kind, Ben and Clint were children. Tough ones, maybe, and hardgrown, but still far too simple and small to stand up with such as Nathan Stark. He would stand alone, and still stand alone, long after Ben and Clint Allison were two Texas cowboys lost in the traildust of time and ten thousand other shadow riders from the Rio Grande.

And this was the man who had asked Nella Torneau to be his wife.

"What," said Ben Allison, the heaviness of his thoughts weighting the question, "did you tell him?"

"I told him," said Nella, the sudden caress in her low voice as soft as the closing touch of her slim hand on his arm, "that I wouldn't trade all the gold in Alder Gulch, nor cows enough to fill ten Gallatin Valleys, for the little piece of Texas I already owned."

"*Texas?*" said Ben uncertainly. "I allow I—"

"Six foot four of it, Ben," she broke in softly. "*Dust-dirty and not a dollar in its dumb-slow pockets.*"

Chapter Twenty

ON THE THIRD NIGHT'S DRIVE from the Tongue they crossed the Little Horn, or East Fork of the Big Horn. There was no trouble at the crossing. Early the fourth night they drove on. In the whole way there had been no sign of pursuit by the Sioux.

At twilight of the fifth day Clint rode in for supplies and a fresh horse. He had ridden the little sorrel into the ground, covering both sides of the Bozeman Road as far as the Big Horn and ten miles beyond. He had seen a few old pony tracks, a few sun-dried droppings, but no signal smoke, tipi-fire coals or other fresh sign that the Sioux had headed them. "If the bastards are after you," he told Ben, "they're trailin' *behind* the herd, waitin' on somebody or suthin' I cain't figger. I kin guarantee you they ain't in front of you though."

Reassured, Ben ordered the cattle rested that night, gave up the night trailing, next morning put the herd back on regulation day drives. Within six hours of sunup, he had company.

Chickasaw spotted them first, a small bunch briefly silhouetted on a butte four miles off and paralleling the herd to the south. Waco saw the next bunch, more of them this time, closer in, moving along a hogback ridge two miles north of the road. By nightfall a dozen bands had been seen numbering from ten to fifty braves and all riding the same way—their way.

They seemed in no hurry and to be keeping no particular watch on the mile-long line of the Texas longhorns. All the same they were heading west with the herd, passing it steadily on the way. That night Clint did not come in and Ben's thoughts were anything but optimistic.

The next day was the same. And the next two following. More Indians and constantly more Indians drifted the buttes and hogbacks paralleling the roughening track of the Bozeman Road. None came closer than a cautious mile from the herd, all acted as though they didn't notice it was there. But with nightcamp of the seventh day from the Little Horn and with the parent stream a short day's drive ahead, Ben and his scowling cowboy crew estimated they had tallied no less than one thousand mounted Sioux in the past seventy-two hours

—and not an old man, squaw or cradleboard papoose among them.

That night Clint rode in again.

"I didn't come sooner," he grinned, " 'cause I reckoned you could see as good as me thet you was crawlin' with Injun lice from brisket to b-hole."

"What're they up to, Clint?" said Ben bluntly.

Clint lost his grin. "Dunno, old salt. It's what's got me scratchin'. I laid up in some rocks fur side of the Big Horn all day yestidday, figgerin' to catch 'em settin' another squeeze like they tried on the Tongue."

"No sech luck?"

"Not nohow. They kept right on goin'. Crossed over above and below the road and never come nigh it."

"Whut you think?"

"Dunno rightly. One thing, sure. They got a taste of them Rollin' Blocks back yonder and whut's more, a good look at 'em. Thet fust scramble, below Reno, they didn't know whut was hittin' 'em. Now they do, brother."

"Reckon thet's why they ain't aimin' to try another river play," grunted Ben.

"I reckon. My idee is thet they've got a better spot picked sum'ers yonder. I seen powerful rough country startin' in beyond the river. Real mountain stuff with a bad, narrer trail in spots I figger, Ben. I'll leave you know fer sure, nuther three, four days."

"Them's the Snow Mountains," Ben told him. "Stark was tellin' me about 'em. He knows this road if he don't know nothin' else. Says he allows he kin tell us where to look sharpest."

"So? How's thet?"

"You see two twin peaks loomin' a shade north of west over back of that rough country?"

"Yeah, allow I did," laughed Clint. "They put me in mind of thet blonde in the Black Nugget."

"Figgers," grinned Ben. "Stark says they call 'em the Squaw Tits."

"They call 'em right." Clint flashed back the grin. "They're a real set of risin' beauties."

Ben went on, no grin now. "There's a big medder footin' 'em on this side. The road crosses it. She's a fair deep dry-cut comin' in off our side and a four-mile canyon goin' out the other."

"Bottled both ends?" frowned Clint.

"Bottled," nodded Ben. "And no grass nor water to carry a

129

drive around her, either side. Accordin' to Stark we got to go through the son of uh bitch and accordin' to my Injun blood the damn Sioux knows it."

"Sounds real interestin'," drawled Clint. "I'll give 'er a looksee. Saleratus—!"

He turned toward the chuckwagon.

"You got thet grub sacked yet?"

Saleratus moved toward them, bulking black against the backing fire. He handed Clint the bulging floursack. The youngster took it, hefted it, laughed softly. "Fer Christ' sake, Saleratus, I ain't goin' ter be gone the hull winter."

"Ya never know," grumped Saleratus. "Leastways you won't die of hunger."

"Sal," said Clint, soberly putting his big hand on the dour cook's grease-sweated shoulder, "alongside yer biscuits, Injun lead ain't in it. A man kin live through two thousand mile of yer potomain poisonin' ain't no two-day ride of Sioux bellyache goin' to cramp him none."

He turned to go, stepping toward the sorrel mare which, a week rested and grass-fat again, he had asked the night wrangler to catch-up for him.

Then, for no reason at all, he did a strange thing. Something Ben couldn't remember him ever having done before. He came back to Ben and held out his hand.

Ben took it, gripping it hard. He felt the sudden, cold sink in his belly as he did. Then Clint grinned awkwardly, pulled his hand away in quick embarrassment, swung up on the little mare and was gone.

They crossed the Big Horn, turning northwest for the Yellowstone, still driving by day, corraling and picket riding by night. They crossed Pryor's Fork of the Yellowstone on the 7th, Clark's Fork on the 15th. Ahead now, the twin granite Squaws' thrust up beyond the horizon. Ben scowled and thought of Clint, and counted the days he had been gone.

For the following five days he drove the men and the herd mercilessly. But with dusk of the 21st, and the cattle bedded outside the throat of the hill-choked entrance of the road's channel into Snow Mountain Meadow, he waited by the fire in vain and long past midnight for the sound of pony hoofs from the west.

At two o'clock, the old moon cradled low and lopsided between the ragged peaks, Ben stood up. Clint had been gone a day short of three weeks. The Indian part of Ben's mind knew what that meant. But the other part wouldn't believe it.

A white man had to see—and be shown.

And somebody had to ride point.

He left the note, scrawled with the stub of his tally pencil on the back of an Arbuckle's bag, pinned to the tailgate of the chuckwagon where Saleratus couldn't miss it when he rolled out at 4:00 A.M. The note wasn't any longer than the pencil—*"Gone to look for Clint"*—and was unsigned.

The late moon hung its dying lantern over the wagon ruts of the Bozeman, giving a man all the light he needed to keep the black on a trail-gait lope. By five o'clock the gelding was beginning to falter and want to quit, and the clouds of the coming day to pinken-up along their lowering underbellies to the east behind him. He let the horse down into a shuffle walk the last mile of the road into the meadow, knowing he would be wise to save some of him for daylight.

Five minutes later he was breaking into the meadow, free of the high hills guarding the road into it, and seeing across its five-mile flats the twin upthrust of the towering Squaws.

In the early light and quiet of the windstill morning, Snow Mountain Meadow lay before him, one of those high, lush, hidden pockets of mountain loveliness which only a traildriver with two thousand miles of rock and sand and bone-dry dust behind him could appreciate to its creek laced, thick grassed fullest. In all its vast, empty amphitheatre, only the clean rush and bubble of the creeks and the nodding wave of the tall mountain hay gave movement to its placid breast.

But above that peaceful floor, high above it, wheeling and circling away from its eerie high on the shoulder of the southern Squaw, spiraling swiftly down toward a creekside copse of alder and mountain laurel in midmeadow, something else was moving.

Ben saw the vulture launch its flight in the same moment the black gelding brought him free of the eastern hills. He followed its long glide, waited a moment longer to check its terminal circle over the midmeadow trees.

Letting the gelding take his own gait toward the grove, he angrily fought back the first thought that rode up in him. Damn his Comanche mind anyhow. It could be anything: an old bear kill, an abandoned, starved wagon mule, a dead Indian campdog, any one of a dozen things other than what a man's Indian blood was hammering at him.

Slowing the black as the road entered the timber, he nodded with the last relieving thought. One thing was certain, anyway. It wasn't a fresh kill. That buzzard knew where he was going. He had been there before.

The last thought was the right one. It was not a fresh kill. Clint had been dead a week.

He saw him as the road bent sharply past a thick stand of laurel to veer across the creek. They had driven an eight-foot sapling into the soft earth, squarely in the center of the wagon ruts. Across the main pole they had lashed a four-foot crossarm. From this, Clint's gaunt body hung in final, grotesque rest.

Ben halted the black, his pale eyes automatically detailing the rest of it.

They had not mutilated him, at least not what a man could see of him. Beyond him stood his sorrel mare, rib-sunken and staring eyed but alive, and picketed with a length of Sioux horsehair rope. Where the starving pony stood, the grass had been eaten to the bare earth, and beyond the range of the picket rope a man could see where the Sioux had cut further armfuls of the rich meadow hay with their hunting knives. Then, while the meaning of that was coming to him, Ben saw the mound of empty Colt cartridges piled carefully at Clint's feet, and the neat row of the five buckskin "warbags" circling the shells.

With that, a man almost *knew*, was legging off his horse and going forward to make last and final sure.

That last thing had been the first to strike him when he broke around the bend. A man had left it until last simply because he had thought he didn't have to look under it to know what *wasn't* there.

Resting on the sagging shoulders of the dead Texas youth, covering his head, leering vacantly at you with its empty eye sockets, was a bonewhite buffalo skull—the exact counterpart of the one found east of Timpas Creek those long months gone.

There was the red hand, the broken gun, the yellow-ocher throat-cut line, all of it. A fifteen-foot billboard printed in circus colors and the King's English, and signed by a scrupulous, Spencerian hand, could not have told a man any clearer or quicker who had killed his brother.

Or who was waiting to do as much for *him*.

It was Crazy Horse.

Ben lifted the buffalo skull away then, hating to touch it, hating to look beneath it—but having to.

It was the way he had thought it would be. The way, in that last minute, that his Kwahadi blood had read the sign of

132

the picketed pony, the empty cartridges, the five Sioux warbags.

They had not scalped him, and his face and throat were unmarked.

Ambushed in the open, with no rock larger than a man's head to hide behind, no tree thicker than a girl's arm to put his back to, Clint had got down five Oglala braves before the blunthead buffalo arrow that was still in him had been driven to its feathers through his back. He had died a warrior's death and the Sioux had given him a warrior's due: the personal warbags of the braves he had taken with him, the powder-burned shells with which he had taken those braves, his pony picketed by his side with ample cut feed and clean water to bear his departed master on the long journey into *Wanagi Yata*, the Sioux Land of the Big Shadow. And they had left him his hair, the highest tribute of Sioux respect for great bravery.

Only his matched stag handled Colts were missing from among the trophies of last honor at his feet. Ben saw that and understood it. Human nature had its limits, even the inhuman variety owned by the Sioux. Two such wonderful specimens of "The Little Guns That Speak Six Times" would be of more use to a living chief than a dead cowboy, warrior's due, or no. The devout Crazy Horse had no doubt paused to pray over the trespass. But the guns were gone.

Ben hid in the grove all day, not daring to leave it in broad light. Between constant glances across the five-mile open of the meadow, he worked the hours away gathering creekstones and piling them by a shallow sinkhole he had found among the alders.

When the sun was low and red-fading over the Squaws, he cut the hardened rawhide bindings from Clint's wasted arms, carried him into the trees.

He laid him in the shallow depression, arranging his neckerchief and worn Levi jacket with rough, big-fingered tenderness. At the last moment he felt in his own cowhide vest, dug out the crumpled banknote Stark had made out to Clint. He tucked it in the frayed denim pocket, stood back, head bowed, looking at his brother. "Like you said, Clint—" he said it clearly and aloud—*"over yonder where the Bozeman peters out."*

With the last stone rolled carefully into place, he returned to the clearing. Cutting the horsehair rope, he led the little sorrel away, bringing her to a weary, spraddle-legged stand over the mounded stones. A man hated to do it, but she was too far starved to live anyway. And besides, her carcass would give the carrion eaters something to take their minds off Clint. He brought out the Kwahadi knife, ripped it with quick mercy across the great vein in her throat. She went down without a sound, gratefully and slowly to the waiting rocks. "You'll keep the coyotes off'n him till spring," said Ben, thick voiced. He turned quickly away and did not look back.

In the clearing, he swung up on the restless black. He gathered the reins, glanced for the last time toward the silent alders.

"Don't spend it all in one place, boy," he muttered brokenly, and heeled the black eastward, out of the grove.

As he went, all understanding of the Indian way, all allowances for its child-simple chivalry, left his heart. They were left in the grove with Clint. Underneath those rocks. In the torn shred of his poor hands, where the buzzards had been at them. In the grimace twisted onto his swollen face by the rupturing shaft of the broadhead arrow in his back.

In Ben Allison's heart, as he raced the black back along the moondark miles of the Bozeman Road, there was only a great, aching emptiness; an emptiness closing slowly and for the last time around the lonely memory of Clint's faraway smile and wild, soft laugh.

And in place of that heartsick emptiness, starting now to pulse through him with thick, soundless fury, an endless, cold anger began to grow.

Chapter Twenty-One

BEN GOT INTO CAMP about ten o'clock. Stark, Waco, Chickasaw and Nella were waiting up for him. He told them briefly about Clint, said nothing about the buffalo skull or Crazy Horse. The peculiar light in his pale eyes forbade both sympathy and pointed inquiry, and by common, uneasy consent they let him do the talking. With his cold beans and bitter, reboiled coffee down, he turned to Stark.

"Time fer questions and answers," he said bluntly. "How would *you* go about gittin' three thousand cattle through Snow Mountain Medder and one thousand Sioux?"

Stark dropped his gaze, stared for a full minute into the fire.

In the big Montanan's mind, many months, many miles, were turning swiftly. He thought of his blunder in seeking a western passage in the deserts of Utah. Of three horses roped together with Texas lariats, fighting out from behind an Arkansas riverbluff and into a high plains blizzard against his advice. Of his counsel to take the Sedalia Trail and of its following Jayhawk trap below the Kansas line. Of his insistence on driving north through Colorado, without turning back to Leavenworth and its Rolling Block rifles. Of his decision to let the Sioux have the stolen cattle below Fort Reno and his judgment, which had led to Curley's death, in trying to winter-camp at Kearney. Of the lethal wisdom in his careless leaving of the whiskey for Clint. And lastly he thought of the lean, darkfaced Texan crouched across the fire and waiting now.

Suddenly, Nathan Stark was not so sure of himself. He had held his cards too close, and too long. The blanket was down, the chips all in the middle of it, right where he had wanted them all along. But with the next-to-last hand laid down and his turn to deal coming up, he knew he did not have the power to raise or call. Quietly, almost humbly, he passed.

"I'd ask Ben Allison," he said.

Ben studied him, said nothing. He swung quickly on Chickasaw.

"Chickasaw?"

The old cattleman shifted his quid, drowned a fire-edge ember.

"I'd ask Mr. Stark to leave me know whut Ben Allison told him."

"Waco?"

"I'll play those."

"All right," said Ben.

He turned back to Stark.

"It's fifteen mile through these hills inter the medder. Five across it. Four out the canyon on the fur side. Thet's twenty-four mile."

"At least," nodded Stark.

"How does the land lay where she opens out of the canyon?"

"Fairly level and wide open. It's a downhill drive all the way to the Yellowstone," answered Stark.

"No more hills or narrer spots?"

"Not till just this side of the river."

Ben's eyes lit up. "How fur this side?"

"About a mile."

"How's she lay at thet spot? The road, I mean."

"Passes between two ridges that funnel toward the river. Where the road leaves the ridges to open out into the Yellowstone bottoms, they're no more than two hundred yards apart."

"Thet's the place then, by God."

"For what, Ben? You've lost me again, man."

"To let 'em hit us!"

"Good God, no! Once we're in that funnel we're worse off than we are here!"

"Not the way I figger it," snapped Ben.

"How do *you* figger it?" drawled Chickasaw acidly.

"Happen you was a Sioux, Chickasaw," said Ben, "how'd you work up a ambush in thet funnel?"

"W'al, lessee, now. Fust off, I'd bottle up the narrer end with about two thirds of my bucks laid up to jump us when we tried comin' out fer the river. Then I reckon I'd take the other third and lay 'em up on this end of the funnel, split fifty-fifty 'twixt the two ridges. Thet's so's soon as we got the critters all inter the funnel they could jump our butts and drive us out the river-end and right inter the main bunch of their boys as was waitin' there."

"Chickasaw," said Ben. "You ain't all white."

"Got a sixteenth Cherokee sum'ers on my daddy's side," drawled the weathered hand. "How's she look to you Comanches?"

136

"I'll let you know when we're out of the other end of Four-Mile Canyon."

"You mean 'if,' don't you?"

"I allus say whut I mean," grunted Ben.

The little moment of lightness was gone now. The big Texan's dark face was once more expressionless. He stood up.

"Waco, would you say the cattle was purty dry?"

"W'al, they ain't drippin'. Last water we had was Bush Crick, yestidday. They sure ain't suckin' none off'n this goddam dead grass we got 'em on here. I'd say there'd best be good water and lots of it in thet medder of yers, yonder."

"Ordinarily you'd say right," muttered Ben.

"Whut you mean?"

"Thet there's more water yonder than *six thousand* cattle could soak up all winter."

"So?" scowled Chickasaw, breaking in.

"So," replied Ben cryptically, "we ain't goin' to let the last calf tech a son of uh bitchin' drop of it!"

"Gawd Amighty, boy! What you got in mind?"

"A night-drive. Right now, Round 'em up."

"First light will ketch us in the medder, boy," the old man objected.

"Iffen it does," growled Ben, "we're dead."

"Meanin'?" It was Waco, again.

"We ain't dead," said Ben.

"See here, Ben," Stark broke in earnestly. "What *are* you getting at? I'm damned if I follow you."

"You're damned if you don't!" rasped Ben.

"Good Lord, Ben, talk sense—!"

Ben nodded, cutting in on him, deep-voiced. "You'd best ketch-up yer longest legged wagonmules, Mr. Stark. Or you and yer precious freight wagons are goin' to be a long time burnin' in Snow Mountain Medder. We're pullin' out."

Ben's camp breaking orders to the hurriedly rolled-out cowboys, were chillingly short: either they got the herd out of Four-Mile Canyon by daybreak or they had wasted six months' wages—not to mention a lot of long Texas hair which would look just dandy drying over a Sioux-lodge smokehole!

It meant making five more miles in six hours of pitchdark than they had been able to make in the best ten-hour, daylight drive they had put behind them since leaving Fort Worth. It meant shoving three thousand cattle that were bone dry and bawling for water twenty-four miles before dawn. It meant putting them across a clear mountain stream of the

best water in Montana on the way, and not losing five minutes to let them drink doing it. And it meant, at last, in terms
of Texas arithmetic simple enough for any bowlegged, Lone
Star mathematician to tot up without his hardboiled trailboss's help, averaging four miles an hour through cut up, narrow pass, new country, with a mile-long mill of pear-thicket
longhorns that were already half wild for water and mean-
hard to handle.

It was a Texas sized order.

By 2 A.M., hazing the tiring drag into the lush bowl of
Snow Mountain Meadow, they had filled the first half of it.

Ahead lay Snow Mountain Creek and Four-Mile Canyon.
Facing the prospect across the darkened meadow, Chickasaw
cursed and spurred his panting gray up to Ben. "Goddam it,
boy, we ain't goin' to quite cut 'er. The fresh-dropped calves
and the nursin' vealers are startin' to straggle out and drop
like flies off'n a stricknyne wolfbait. And them goddam lead
steers are smellin' crickwater and wantin' to run. We cain't
hold 'em, boy. Whut're we goin' to do?"

"Let 'em run!" gritted Ben. Then, bellowing it into the
darkness. "Tex! Tex Anderson—"

"Here!" The bearded cowboy drove his pony up through
the boiling ground-dust. "How you want 'em headed, Ben?"

"Fast!" rapped Ben. "Me and Chickasaw and my point
boys here will cut on ahead and git set over in the mouth of
the canyon. You and the rest of the boys git on the drag and
shove the sons uh bitches fer the crick on the hightail. You
got to pile 'em inter thet water so fast they cain't stop, and
not so fast we cain't stop 'em on the fur side. You hear,
boy?"

"Shove off!" shouted Tex. "I'm gone."

Ben swung the black, yelling for Waco, Hogjaw, Slim and
Charley Stringer to let the leaders go and to follow him and
Cherokee "on the busted run."

The six ponies bunched up, hammering down the road toward the midmeadow crossing. Behind them, the first steers
were already hoisting their stiffened tails and rattling the
ground with the dry clack of their excited trot. Ben led his riders across the stream on a digging run for the yawning canyon ahead. He split them three-and-three, he and Chickasaw
and Waco taking the right wing, the others the left.

"Try and turn 'em in when they hit you!" he yelled across
to Hogjaw. "We won't be pickin' our noses on this side."

"I gotcha!" echoed Hogjaw.

"Fer Gawd's sake," roared old Chickasaw, "don't nobody git in front of them!"

"Jest whut I had in mind!" hollered Hogjaw, acidly. "You goddam ol' mossyhorn, who the hell you think you're ridin' with? The Fo't Wuth Baptist Ladies Auxiliary?"

"Fork you!" yowled the old man, angrily. "I was ropin' and th'owin' rangebull-stuff when you wasn't straddlin' nothin' wilder'n a wet bedsheet, you banty-legged leetle bastard!"

"Shet up and spread out!" yelled Ben. "Yonder they come."

It went slick. Slicker than a man dared hope.

They got the leaders turned and chuted into the canyon, and the main herd jamming in behind them, five minutes after the first steers blundered up through the dark. After that there wasn't anything to it but to lay back and join the other boys in shouting and rope-whipping the drag in after them. By two-thirty the last stumbling heifer was on her way down Four-Mile Canyon, with the first hitch of Stark's wagonmules hard on her lagging heels.

At four o'clock the first steer broke out of the canyon's mouth onto the vast plateau of the Middle Yellowstone. By five, the last of Stark's supply and freight wagons were a clean mile beyond the canyon wall. They had made it.

Ben, hanging back in a brushy water-cut with Chickasaw and Waco, watched the wagon train follow the herd over a distant swell of the plateau and drop out of sight toward the Yellowstone. He flicked his glance back to the sharpening silhouettes of the ridges buttressing the canyon exit behind them, waiting for what the coming daylight should show them along those ridges—*happen he had been right.*

Ten minutes later the clearing wash of the daylight, filtering westward and around the backsides of the two Squaws, showed him and his silent companions a sight few white men have lain on their bellies in the brush to see; and lived to laugh about: hundreds and hundreds of Sioux horsemen, dot-small with the distance and the morning dimness, filing down out of the canyon's flanking ridges, north and south, and streaming off to the west to disappear, within bare minutes and their own angry dust, beyond the bulge of the prairie.

"Ben," said Chickasaw soberly, "yore eyes are younger'n mine. Whut you see along them yonder ridges which them red bastards jest come down off'n?"

"Oldtimer," murmured the tall Texan, "fur as I kin see,

piled up there along them ridges, ten days deep, there ain't nothin' but hot Injun hoss manure."

"Amen," said Waco, rolling to his feet. "They shore frittered away a bad week waitin' fer Little Ben Allison and his boys in Snow Mountain Medder."

They went for their horses then. Chickasaw swung up last. He was still looking back toward the fading Sioux dust. When he turned to Ben, his eye-corners weren't crinkling anymore.

"I allow I never thought you could do it, boy, bringin' the herd through so far, so fast and ketchin' them Sioux asleep like we done back yonder. They's one thing troublin' me, all the same. Ain't we jest put it off by one more drive?"

"You mean the massacree, old hoss?"

Ben actually grinned it.

Old Chickasaw scowled, looked sharply at him. True, it was a nippy November morning, not all the frost being on the buffalo grass, and some little of it touching the corners of the big trailboss's mouth. All the same, happen you had spent some years along the North Concho and could read Comanche sign, it was a grin.

"Sure funny, ain't it," Chickasaw growled irritably.

Ben kneed the black toward him, reached his hand and laid it on the bony old shoulder.

"Chickasaw," he said, the grin disappearing but the frost not going with it, "happen old Ka-dih is still on my side, the joke'll be on Crazy Hoss this time." Then, quietly, as he turned the black to follow the wagons. "These happy little Oglala bastards ain't begun to learn how uncommon hard a Comanche kin laugh at suthin' thet's real funny—"

With the pause and the sudden ugliness in the words, he laughed. It was a short, bad sound, and Chickasaw exchanged narrow glances with Waco.

"Yeah, suthin' thets *real* funny," repeated Ben Allison slowly. "Like whut they done to Clint!"

Chapter Twenty-Two

THEY SAW NO MORE of the Sioux that morning, nor all of the long afternoon. Which proved nothing. The slope of the plateau toward the Yellowstone, despite Stark's description of it as "wide open and fairly level," was one of those pieces of high prairie which waves like an ocean. A flanking swell of low, east-west ridges paralleled the trail for miles, and the Indians could have been moving their whole nation west and never shown a travois pony in the process. Adding to that discomfort, the ground cover of the plateau shortly turned to the matted, close curl of true buffalo grass and wouldn't raise a decent dust if you drove a locomotive through it.

They did not dare attempt a noonhalt because of the condition of the cattle. It was all they could do to hold them on the trail and keep them moving. To have stopped and let them spread would have been to tempt the disaster of not being able to get them gathered and going ahead again. It was a ticklish piece of timing Ben was trying to achieve, too, anyway you look at it.

He knew, from Stark's telling him, that the river was a scant ten miles from the outlet of Four-Mile Canyon. Normally, it would have meant about a three or four o'clock drive, but the plan that was turning in the big Texan's mind demanded that they bring the herd into Stark's "funnel" just at sunset.

The Indians had two favorite times of day for working on white men: early morning, late afternoon.

Their morning schedule had already been frustrated by Ben's unprecedented, twenty-four-mile night drive. Now a man wanted to give them all the time they might feel they needed to get ahead of the herd and into their last chance positions behind the converging lines of the funnel ridges. At the same time, he wanted to hold his thirst-driven herd as long on the trail as he could. The plan also called for that, and in capital letters.

At two o'clock they sighted the winding, dark line of naked cottonwoods watermarking the distant Yellowstone. At the same time the wind, dead and waiting all day long, began to stir the two-inch curl of the buffalo grass—from the west, and from the river.

Feeling it fresh and clean on his sweating face, Ben

141

shouted to the swing riders, stood in his stirrups and waved frantically to those following the drag.

With his signal, the cowboys swung their ponies wide of the staggering cattle, raced them forward. They could feel that river wind as quick as Ben, and read its meaning without his yell and wave. Even as they spurred their mounts to head the herd, the first steers were flinging up their heads, beginning to break into a stumbling trot.

In as many seconds as there were desperate riders ringing them, all the cattle were getting their caked noses up and following the leaders. Another two or three minutes and the whole herd would have been running, but Ben had moved in scant time. With all twenty-five fulltime riders in front of them, racing their mounts across the point and the forward shoulders of the swing, the run for the river was forestalled.

By four o'clock, with the Yellowstone but three miles ahead and the spreading wings of Stark's funnel beginning in less than a mile, even Saleratus, his Mexican campboys, the night wrangler and Nathan Stark, himself, were cowboying with the best of them. And needing to. It was all, and maybe more than all, that they or any other thirty men could do to hold the bellowing cattle back.

Everything now depended on their ability to do so for the next forty-five minutes, or until they had every head deep into the funnel.

There was a thirty-first rider in that yelling, cursing, wild riding point those last endless minutes before the river. But she was not on the company payroll and didn't count—except to Ben Allison and her other twenty-five big-hatted Texas worshippers.

If Ben and the men had thought the girl was something through the Red River rains, or the Platte Valley heat, or the six hundred miles of cowboy toil up the Sioux-ridden Bozeman, they hadn't yet begun to know Nella Torneau.

"Goddam it, Ben!" yelled old Chickasaw, "git thet crazy gal back in the wagons 'fore she kills herse'f! She's runnin' in on them steers like she was out to bust a rodeo record or suthin'. Lookee there! Lookit thet, by Gawd! You see her run thet goddam paint mare of hers square inter thet dun steer was beginnin' to run yonder? Jesus Christ! She knocked him plumb on his goddam butt. Git her out'n here!"

"He needed knockin'," yelled Ben. "Leave her be. She's wuth a roundup crew. Goddamit, she's got all the boys ridin' clean over their fool heads tryin' to keep up with her and
142

look good. Christ! You ever in yer life see sech a girl, Chick-asaw!"

"Not in mine, nor nobody else's!" bellowed the old cow-boy. "Watch it on yer right, boy!" he shouted suddenly. "Thet roan bull, yonder!"

Ben spun the black, couldn't head the big six-year-old herdbull that had broken past Waco and was running for the river. He flashed the .44, threw two shots from the hip into him, quartering away. The bull bawled piteously, buck-jumped sideways, crashed into the dirt of the wagon road, his broken neck doubled under him. The point of steers following him out of the herd broke their starting run, split around his sprawling carcass, hesitated to sniff curiously at it. Waco and Hogjaw Bivins were in front of them then, their cutting horses moving like eight-hundred-pound cats. They got them bunched, hammered them back. The herd rumbled ahead, unbroken.

A short four hundred yards west now, the funnel narrowed for its slightly north-twisting exit into the Yellowstone bot-toms. The bottoms themselves were hidden by the turn, though less than half a mile distant.

It was now or never.

Ben waved up Chickasaw and Waco. With the three lath-ered ponies held down to an excited, side-dancing lope, the in-cessantly bellowing cattle crowding up on their nervous rumps, the conversation of their tightjawed riders was necessarily suc-cinct.

"You all clear on it now, boys?" said Ben.

"You ride ahead, up yonder ridge," barked Waco. "If the Sioux are set and waitin' like you reckon them to be, you wave three times. If they ain't, you wave onct."

"If we git the three waves," growled Chickasaw, "meanin' they're out there 'twixt us and the river, ev'rybody pulls out from in front of the herd and follers you up the ridge."

"That's it," said Ben. "All set?"

"Cain't wait," shrugged Waco caustically. "I only hope yer second guess is better'n yer fust. Dammit, Ben! We ain't seen hide nor hair on them Sioux you figgered would bottle our butts onct we had the hull outfit inter the funnel."

"I reckon Waco's got suthin' there, boy," old Chickasaw scowled. "She ain't pannin out square on yer leetle skedjool so fur."

Ben stood in his stirrups, looking quickly back across the herd. They saw his pale eyes narrow just ahead of the wolf-spread of the grin.

"Ain't it?" he rasped, dropping back into the saddle. "Grab another look, boys. Tell me whut you see sproutin' them ridge-tops back yonder."

Waco and Chickasaw twisted around. They did not need to stand in their stirrups. The late sunlight was fresh and clean along the ridges behind them, and it was to their backs, not bothering the widening squint of their eyes in the least.

"They ain't turkey feathers," was the laconic way Waco chose to put it.

"Nor yet barnyard chicken," agreed Chickasaw with equal prairie savoir faire. "I'd hazard they was mainly eagle," if there was such a thing as a hurried Texas drawl, Chickasaw was hurrying one, "with mebbe a small hatch of hawk th'owed in fer the pure hell of it."

For a "hazard," the weathered Texan's opinion was a pure-good guess.

Lining both ridgetops, motionless as so many red cameos against the slant of the late sun, were no less than three hundred mounted Sioux. And even as the three cowboys saw them and Ben was shouting the warning back to Hogjaw and Charley Stringer, the hostile horsemen were sweeping down the ridges onto the level track of the Bozeman Road below.

The herd was sealed off. Right on schedule.

"I will see you boys in Sunday school," said Ben Allison, and sent the black gelding in a cat-scramble up the ridge.

Minutes later he was atop the hills, seeing beyond him the sparkling, snow water sweep the Yellowstone. And seeing, on this side of it, what thirty-one Texas lives depended on. And on the long-odds chance of which he had gambled those lives.

As Chickasaw was wont to say in his moments of rare sentiment for his jockey-sized friend, Waco Fentriss, "There could be a leetle more of it, but it couldn't be put together no better."

Crazy Horse could not have lined his braves up any more perfectly if he had consulted Ben beforehand.

There were maybe six hundred of them between the funneling outlet of the Bozeman Road and the river. The Sioux chief had them spread in a quarter-mile semicircle, his center based on the road, his flanks cupping toward the ridge upon which Ben sat the gelding. And had Ben been able to understand Sioux, and Crazy Horse's voice been equal to spanning the distance between them, the Sioux leader could not have shouted his intentions any more clearly.

Tashunka Witko knew he had all the red power in that

part of Montana either mounted up behind him or presently closing off the herd's rear. He knew the Ride-A-Heaps had no chance at all this time. And that he could afford the luxury of hitting them head-on, to finish it once and for all in real north plains style. He knew why he had trailed them four hundred miles, and he knew why it wasn't going to be necessary to trail them another four hundred yards.

When the army had started its string of forts across the Powder River Treaty Land, Crazy Horse had known what it meant to him and to his people: the coming of the settler, the killing off of the buffalo, the end of the Indian. He had known then, as he knew now, what he had to do about that and what he would do about it. The Sioux had to close the Bozeman Road for all time. He knew that they had had it closed, too, until these cursed Ride-A-Heaps and their bad-smelling spotted buffalo had dared what the entire United States Army had not—to break it wide open again, Sioux or no Sioux.

He knew, finally, when word came to him in the war-camp on the Tongue, that the Texas cowboys had pushed their great herd past Fort Kearney in the dead of night, that Wakan Tonka, the Sioux Great Spirit, had touched him, Tashunka Witko, upon the shoulder.

And he knew that Crazy Horse was chosen from among all his people to strike these invaders into the bloody dirt of the Bozeman, to show their craven white brothers what the Dakota People meant when they made their sacred mark on a treaty paper, and to close the Thieves Road forever.

Indeed, Tashunka Witko knew many things. In all his lonely, skyswept empire there were perhaps but two small things he did not know.

Ben Allison for one.

And the way of three thousand thirst-crazed Texas longhorns with whatever might stand between them and their first water in seventy-two hours, for another.

In the last minute, Crazy Horse saw Ben on the ridge. The Sioux chief's eyes were as good as any cowboy's. His memory maybe even better.

He knew Ben at once.

He jumped his piebald roan stallion out into the open road, fifty yards ahead of his warriors. He slid him on his hocks, reared him up in a forehoof-lashing stand. He held his rifle high above his head in both hands, shaking it at Ben. His deep-throated Oglala shout rolled across the open ground and up the ridge. *"Tshaoh! Tshaoh!"* Then, up-ending the rifle, he fired four shots into the air, spun the wiry little stallion back towards his waiting braves.

Ben's mouth twisted.

The rifle, held up in both hands, meant the chief was letting him know he had Big War on his mind. The four shots meant he was enlisting, after his devout fashion, Wakan Tonka's blessing in the bloody matter. Four, Pawnee Perez had told Ben at Fort Kearney, was the Sioux Good Medicine number. When they used it on you, you were to look out right sharp, for it meant they figured they had you where your hair was short and you couldn't get loose without leaving your scalp.

Perez had also told him another number. One the Sioux hated. Five. A very big number. Very bad medicine number. By a heap the worst they knew how to count to.

Ben flung up his Henry, both hands high with it. Then he dropped its buttplate to his hip, levered the five shots into the clouding sunset overhead.

With that, he was standing in his stirrups, black hat in hand, checking for the last time the bawling mill of the vast herd below and behind him.

The cattle were crazy now. They were piling and jamming into the thin line of riders fronting them, their swollen tongues lolling, their alkali-crusted eyes rolling wildly. They were riding the rumps of the steers fronting them, goring right and left with their four-foot horns, crushing down their weaker fellows, driving them underfoot, bellowing in a cracked and hideous bawl their wildness for the water they could smell but not see.

"Let 'em go!" screamed Ben. And flagged the black hat three times across the cloud-red stain of the five o'clock sky.

A Texas longhorn can run like a deer, rage like a lion, and fears a man on horseback no more than does a Spanish fighting bull. Three thousand of them, broken out of a two hundred-yard-wide unloading chute in wildeyed, full stampede, insane for water and with nothing between them and that water but a few hundred mounted Indians, is a sight no man forgets.

To Ben and his cheering, rebel yelling cowboys crowding the ridgetop above, it was the finest sight Texas eyes ever beheld.

For certain of the stunned Sioux, to an exact number never really determined, it was the last, worst sight the human eye can hold—the sudden fearful exposure on widened retina, of the skull-grinning picture of coming death.

The distance from the funnel mouth to the river, was no more than four hundred yards. The Sioux had their ambush line set midway. They had only time to look down the hoarsely-lowing throats of the maddened lead steers, and to jam their ponies into a milling tangle of attempted escape, when the following main wave of the stampede struck them.

The Indian ponies, unbroken to the strange smell of the white man's cattle and to the foreign thunder of their harsh bellowing, went crazy.

As usual, the horsemanship of their red masters was superb. Time and again the awestricken cowboys saw its incredible evidence. A feathered brave, off his pony and down and helpless on the ground: a companion riding full gallop under the nose of certain, crushing death, scooping him up to safety and somehow getting the double-mounted pony out of the herd and away. A bonneted chief, knocked or horn-hooked from his pony, bounding up and swing-vaulting to another riderless and loose-galloping mount on the dead, wild run. The bravery and skill of the Sioux were literally unbelievable, and the spell-bound cowboys sat and stared in simple, speechless amazement.

But in the end the herd began to thin, and Crazy Horse to gather his battered forces about him in the slowing dust of its drag.

This was the moment for men from Texas and rifles from Illion Forge, New York.

Ben led the charge down the ridge squarely into them, his riders fanning into a spread line as they bore down on the dismayed Sioux. At a hundred yards they opened with the Rolling Blocks, the effect of the volley instant and deadly at the range and into such close packed ranks. Then the hard-running cowponies were at seventy-five and at fifty yards, and the Remingtons were being jammed back into their saddle scabbards and Colonel Colt was out and speaking extemporaneously on the informal subject of *"Longhorn Stampedes for Water and Hip-shooting Sioux at Forty Feet."*

It was more than red flesh and blood could bear—or intended to.

The Sioux broke it off as short as a buffalo lance in a dead bull's bottom. They streamed away north and south by the tens, the scores, the hundreds. And as they went, Ben's cowboys slipped the Rolling Blocks back out, legged off their horses, hit the ground in bowlegged, offhand stances and continued to pour it on until the last buck was luckily beyond the extreme range of the Remingtons.

Which was something like four hundred yards and five minutes later.

The Battle of the Bozeman Crossing of the Yellowstone was over as of 5:25 P.M., October 23, 1866.

And the only scratch Ben Allison's Texans took in it from start to finish was the one Waco gave himself while celebrating the event by shaving with Chickasaw's straightedge the following morning.

Chapter Twenty-Three

ON THE THIRD DAY west of the Yellowstone the snows, threatening since October and Fort Kearney, began. The morning of the fourth day there was six inches on the ground and the heavy promise of more to come in the sullen clouds to the north.

But the clouds held back. They continued to crouch in respectful place along the horizon of the Three Forks country and the high sourcelands of the Big Muddy, bade, as it were, by old Ka-dih himself, to stand and cry "Halt! enough!" and to let his quarterbred Comanche grandson finish his mighty journey in peace.

Whether it was the will of the venerable Kwahadi god, or the work of a simple, squaw-winter vagary of Montana weather, the 1500-mile hegira of Nathan Stark's great herd ended peacefully.

It was twilight of December 3 when Ben ordered the leaders thrown into a halting mill and the herd bedded on the Emigrant Gulch headlands. Shortly after 10:00 A.M. the following day, the 4th, the point steers ambled out of the gulch's western terminus, led their motley-colored, high-withered followers down upon history and the little settlement of Bozeman, Montana.

Here Stark left the wagons, pushing on with the Texans and the herd around the hills north of Virginia City and so, at last, into the trails-end grasslands of the Gallatin. On his orders, the cattle were moved out across the great valley's floor, to the river. There they were turned loose and scattered, ten miles north and south, along the reaching shelter of the Gallatin's timbered brakes. It was December 8, 1866.

By nightfall of the 9th, Nathan Stark was seated at his desk beyond Esau Lazarus's little green door in the Black Nugget Saloon, paying off his twenty-five hired Texas hands.

To each man he gave, in addition to his regular wages, a $100 bonus, the Remington Rolling Block rifle he had been issued below Fort Kearney, a house-tab for all the whiskey he could personally carry out of the Black Nugget before he himself was carried out of it, and stage fare from the nearest linepoint station in Montana Territory to Fort Worth, Texas. To each, as well, he gave a firm clasp of his tough hand, a steady blue-eyed statement of his personal thanks and obligations, and the expressed hope they would one and all think well of Nathan Stark along any trail the future might see them riding.

It was an impressive thing, this slow passing of awkward, highbooted Texas riders through Esau Lazarus's banking room, seeing them take the big Montanan's hand, not quite knowing what to do with it, stammering, blushing, trying in their rough ways to pass it off as though it was the regular thing to get cash bonuses, gift guns, free whiskey and first-class fare home from just any old cattle drive.

Watching them come and go, from where he and Chickasaw and Waco waited uncomfortably on a spindle-legged settee in the far corner of the little room, Ben swallowed hard. At the same time Waco was digging a bony knuckle into the eye that had offended him at Curly's grave-side and Chickasaw was blowing the creases out of a brand-new backpocket bandanna.

When the last of them had gone, Stark called Chickasaw and Waco over to the desk, handed each of them a Mastin Bank of Kansas City draft for $500. He shook hands with them as he had with the others, soberly asked them not to say anything to their companions about the added bonus. It wasn't that the others didn't deserve every penny as much, he told them, but only that they had backed Ben Allison on every turn from Red River to the Yellowstone. And without Ben's way having prevailed, he guessed that neither he nor anyone else would have to tell them where they and himself and every last head of the San Saba herd would be right now.

Then, at final last, they too were gone, and Ben was alone with Nathan Stark.

They looked at each other a long time, neither faltering in his regard, neither offering to put words to what was in the mind of each. In the end it was Stark who nodded slowly, spoke in his dry, flat voice.

"Well, Ben, what are we going to do about you?"

"I could say what *I* think we're goin' to do, Mr. Stark," he said quietly. "But it's my way to listen fust. You tell me."

"We had a deal," said Nathan Stark.

"We did," said Ben Allison.

"You've always believed I meant it, and would go through with it didn't you, Ben?"

"Likely."

"Your brother never agreed with you."

The shadow darkened Ben's pale eyes only for a moment,

then faded out and was gone. "Clint never believed in nobody, exceptin' mebbe onct in a while me."

"Clint was right, Ben. About not believing in anybody. And about me. He was smart, Clint was. *Real* smart. A lot, lot smarter than you. Did you know that, Ben?"

"I reckon I did, Mr. Stark. Clint allus figgered it was him takin' care of me, stead of the other way around. I allow mebbe in his way he many times was, too. I wasn't never very sharp."

Stark's eye corners wrinkled quickly. His wide mouth bent to one of his dodo-rare, stiffly awkward grins. "God save me," he said, "from ever meeting a sharp Texan."

Ben didn't ask him what he meant. He didn't care. It was hot in the little room and the talk getting way too deep for him.

"I reckon we'd best git on with it," he frowned.

"I reckon we had," agreed Nathan Stark. "What do you want?"

"My third of the herd."

"In money?"

"Greenback cash."

"That wasn't the deal. The deal was one third of whatever the herd earned. It hasn't earned a nickel yet. We could have the biggest die-up ever, with a bad winter. There might not be a steer left alive in the Gallatin, come spring."

"Your gamble," said Ben dryly. "I made mine on the Yellerstone."

"And figure you won it. That it, Ben?"

"Easy."

"I see. What do you figure one third of the herd is worth?"

"Three times what it was in Fort Worth."

Stark looked at him. The herd was worth eight, possibly ten times what it had cost in Texas.

"You're crazy," he said.

"And stickin' to it," nodded Ben quickly.

"You want ten thousand dollars, then?"

"In small bills. Tonight."

"You're a fool, Ben."

"Tell me suthin' ev'rybody don't know. And gimme the money."

"What about Clint's share?"

"He's got it."

"Make sense, Ben."

"I give him your bankdraft, thet's all."

"That doesn't settle anything, man! It was just a piece of paper."

"It does," was all Ben would say. "It was the way Clint wanted it. He asked fer his pay and you give it to him."

Stark shrugged. You couldn't talk business with these Texans. Not the ones like Ben Allison. To them, their word or yours, once given, was the end of the matter. Maybe in his simple, plodding way he was right. Maybe, as he saw it, Clint had been honestly paid off. It didn't make sense, but the longer you knew Ben Allison the more you wondered what *did*. And the more you thought about who was *really* right.

Shaking his head, Stark pulled the desk drawer open; began quickly counting the bills into precise stacks before him.

"Do you know what you're selling for this money, Ben?" he asked.

"One thousand head of San Saba cows," grunted Ben.

"Nothing else?"

"Yeah—my chances of bein' a Montana millionaire."

Stark stopped counting and looked up at him.

"It's a bad deal, Ben."

"Best I ever made," nodded Ben. "Keep countin'."

"What do you mean, 'the best you ever made'?" asked Stark curiously.

Ben knit his brows, fingered his long jaw. It was something that had been turning in his mind for a long time, and he didn't hurry it now.

"Mr. Stark," he said at last, "your kind grows big. Mine allus stays the same size. We don't eat the same grub, you and me, nor we ain't meant to share the same bunk. I could stay in yer Gallatin Valley a hundred years and never learn yer ways nor profit by 'em. We ain't cut from the same stick and we'll never sprout good nor do well in the same soil. Your kind of tree puts roots a mile down, sixty sections square. You pull all the water and sap out'n the ground as fur as you kin reach, and any man thet's tryin' to grow on it alongside of you is goin' to drouth-out and die young."

He paused, the painful lines of the hard-dredged thought easing away.

"I jest reckon," he said quietly, "thet I'd ruther die my own size, and in my own way and time."

Nathan Stark stood up. His wide blue eyes were for once warm. The flat timbre of his voice, in that final minute, fell as softly as Ben's. He handed him the money and Ben took it, standing there uncertainly with it in his hand.

152

"Ben," he said, "you're the only man I ever envied. You're what every man thinks he's going to be when he's a little boy. And wishes he had been when he's an old man. Ten months ago I meant to cut you and your brother into the ground. Six months ago it was the same. And three, and two, and one. You had taken my money from me and I owed you nothing but to get it back in any way I could, and with compound interest. Clint saw that. You never did and you never will. I tried to take the girl from you. You didn't even see that. You won't even see it now that I've told you.

"Ben," he added slowly, "goddam your simple soul and slow, straight mind. You're the only man who ever beat me, or ever will."

He paused, putting out his hand.

"We never did shake hands," he said quietly.

Ben took his hand, let it go quickly, all the strange feeling he held for the big Montanan coming up in him in an embarrassing, tongue-tying wave.

In the little moment he gripped his hand, bringing his pale eyes up to meet the harsh blue ones, he knew what it was about Nathan Stark a man would never forget, or let anybody take away from him. Cold-brainy, hard-dealing, wolf-tough. Call him what you would, and watch him close because of it. Be maybe a little afraid of him, too, and want to get away from him and stay away from him. In the end he was your kind of man and you knew it: *he was a fighting man, pure and simple.*

He turned to go then, and was at the door when Stark's last words caught up to him.

"Sometime, Ben," called the bearded Montanan, "when you want to measure a real big man, step against the nearest wall and make your mark."

"I was never any good," said Ben, "at makin' marks—"

He closed the little green door on the words. He went quickly through the Black Nugget and to the eagerly whickering black gelding at the hitching rail outside it. Swinging up, he turned the gelding into the freezing slush of Van Buren Street, toward the coal-oil lamplight of the Arbor Restaurant, where Nella and the others would be waiting. He did not look back and he never saw Nathan Stark again.

They brought their horses to a stop on the divide, sat them looking back and down on Virginia City.

Ben Allison had been on this skyline and in this wind before. Ten months ago, on a winter night no different from this one, he had reined the black in and gazed down upon the distant, twinkling lights of Alder Gulch and the Grasshopper Diggings.

He had been an outlaw then, a hunted man without money, or friends, or any future longer than the seven-inch barrel of his Army Colt. Now he had all these things—and much, much more.

With the first of the thought he felt, subconsciously, for the strange, thick feel of the moneybelt beneath his wolfskin winter coat, and he looked across the night to where the two cowboys held their ponies, back-hunched to the bite of the wind, waiting to follow him home to Texas, and beyond, into whatever of future he and the trailherd money could make for all of them.

With the last of the thought, he reached in the darkness for Nella's hand. As he found it, the little paint mare sidled closer to the black.

"Penny for your thoughts, Ben," Nella laughed softly.

"Wouldn't sell 'em for all the gold Stark's goin' to make on our cows," smiled the big Texan.

"A kiss then," said Nella, and leaned quickly in the saddle to brush her lips against his dark skinned cheek.

"Thet's a heap different," murmured Ben. "They're cheap at half thet price."

"So, boy—"

"I was thinkin' of suthin' I said to Clint when fust we rode down off'n this same ridge inter Virginy City. I told him I had a hunch we was goin' to make the biggest strike since Comstock stumbled on his lode in Six-Mile Canyon."

His long arm circled her slender shoulders, his drawling southern voice slowed.

"I reckon you're it, Nella girl," he said softly.

"And goddam it!" cut in Chickasaw testily, "*I* reckon thet me and Waco are freezin' our Texas tails. Iffen you two have got done with yer infernal pawin' and rumpin'-up to one another, I got one vote says we put the Petmakers to these here Red River crowbaits and p'int 'em fer Fo't Wuth!"

"Second the motion," complained the diminutive Waco. "I ain't got nobody's love to keep me warm, savin' my own. And she's done froze clean up to my shortribs a'ready."

"Three votes for the Sunny San Saba," laughed Nella Torneau. She reined the little paint around, flashing her old bright smile at Ben. "What do we hear from Comanche County?"

"She's unanymous," grinned Ben. "Three cheers fer the Indypendent Republic of Texas!"

They were gone then, the eager ponies moving quickly down the far slope of the Virginia City stage road and into the waiting southern darkness, the black gelding and the paint mare first, the bony gray and the ewe-necked chestnut last.

"W'al, Chickasaw," drawled Waco, nodding idly toward Ben's lean back, "what you acherally think o' him, now thet ev'rythin's said and did and we're only sixteen hundred miles from home?"

Chickasaw thought it over. He spat contemplatively, and carefully, downwind.

"He'll never amount to nothin' on God's green prairie, exceptin' six foot four of dumb-simple San Saba cowboy," said the old cattleman softly.

Then, more of pride and meaning in it than any book could put in print, or clumsy storyteller spell out:

"He's jest another tall man from Texas—"

* * *

SEVENTY-FIVE MILES SOUTH of Billings is the Cheyenne Agency town of Lame Deer, Montana. Speaking there in the summer of 1915 at a Nathan Stark Memorial Day program arranged by the Society of Montana State Pioneers, the famed Cheyenne chief, Two Moons, then over seventy years old and straight as a sapling pine, had this to say of the Battle of the Bozeman Crossing of the Yellowstone:

"It was a good fight. I was there with my friend, Crazy Horse. We did that in those days, one chief riding with another, like that. No, the Cheyenne were not at war then. But I was there with Tashunka anyway. Like I say. Like a brother.

"Those were great rifles the cowboys had. And those cattle frightened our ponies and made the hearts of Tashunka's Sioux very bad.

"Yes, I remember Stark. He was a big man, heavy and tall, with a yellow beard, I remember, and he rode a fine bay stallion and was a brave fighter.

"I remember another man though. He had no beard and

155

he was darkskinned, almost like an Indian. He had pale hair, too. It was the color of dry corn leaves and covered with a big black hat. He rode in front of the cattle that day. And in front of the cowboys. Crazy Horse knew him and they shook their guns at each other before the cattle ran. That is the one I remember. That one with the big black hat.

"He was the tallest of them all. . . ."
